GETTING OFF

Books by Don Carpenter

HARD RAIN FALLING

BLADE OF LIGHT

THE MURDER OF THE FROGS

GETTING OFF

GETTING OFF

OFF

a novel by
DON CARPENTER

E. P. Dutton & Co., Inc., New York, 1971

Published simultaneously in Canada by
Clarke, Irwin & Company Limited, Toronto and Vancouver

Library of Congress Catalog Card Number: 70-133588

SBN 0-525-11330-4

For Gene and Gerry

GETTING OFF

1

Plover woke up for once in a loving mood and lay on his back blinking his eyes, preparing himself to get up and make some coffee. He remembered it was Sunday and there would be the Sunday paper to read; and then he also remembered that the children were with his parents and would not be back until that afternoon, and so he could turn toward his wife, touch her, pull her still hot with sleep toward him, and make love to her. They seldom made love in the daylight, and he knew she was delighted by the surprise, by the sudden passion; but he felt a slight coldness at his center, as if making love in the daytime was wrong. He knew that if he did reach over for her the feeling would pass as soon as she wrapped herself around him, that the passion would take charge and it would be just what he wanted.

It was nearly always like this. The impulse toward passion would come and then he would think of something or the cold feeling would come into his chest, and so they would either not make love at all, or they would, but it would not be the same as if he had from the first stirring moved toward the climax. But for her sake, for the release of obligation, he did reach out and touch her on the shoulder, and then when he felt her stirring and knew she was half-awake, he moved his body over next to hers and put his hand over her breasts. He kissed her soft hot mouth and then her neck and felt her pull away from him and turn over, away from him, onto the other side of the bed. They had been married fourteen years and nothing like this had ever happened before.

Plover turned over on his back again, his eyes open. He felt angry and frustrated. He knew she was not asleep. If she had been asleep she would have come into his arms, as she always did. She wanted lovemaking more often than he did. If she had been asleep she would have groaned or something. She had been awake and had deliberately turned away from him. It was not her period. That had ended four or five days before. They had made love the night it ended, as they always did, even though it was a little difficult for her. He always felt so guilty about feeling relieved that it was her period that they would always make love then. Plover turned his head and looked over at her. All he could see was a mound of tousled hair and her shape under the thick coverlet. He could tell from the way she was set that she was awake. He threw the covers off himself and got out of bed, tucked her in with false solicitude, pulled on his pants, and left the bedroom, closing the door after himself.

Plover went into the kitchen to make coffee. The kitchen was filthy. There were two or three inches of coffee in the Chemex and so he just turned on the gas and found his favorite mug and washed it out and set it on the cutting board. There was no room on the counter. At his feet three paper sacks bulged with garbage, and a fourth sack was over on its side, contents spilled out, as if one of the cats had knocked it over and rummaged through it. Plover bit his lip with irritation and went out the back door and around the house, down the driveway to where the Sunday paper was lying, hot from the sun, and scarred by concrete. Plover ripped off the string and tossed it into the bushes as he moved slowly up the driveway. There was no morning breeze today. It was going to be hot, at least in Mill Valley and perhaps in the whole Bay Area. It did not matter; he was not going to do anything today.

Back in the kitchen the coffee was ready and he poured a cup and put in milk and sugar and took it into the living room to sip while he read his paper. Plover had been off cigarettes for three months, and it was getting easier all the time to go through this morning ritual without smoking. First he read the front page, which on Sunday never amounted to much but allowed him to sip about half his coffee. Then he would be ready to take the section containing his favorite columnists into the bathroom. Afterward he would come out and finish his coffee rapidly and pour another cup, to be sipped comfortably as he read through the rest of the paper. But this morning he was irritated at his wife, and his bowels were not functioning properly, and so he was still on his first cup of coffee and reading Herb Caen when he heard his wife open the bedroom door and then close the bathroom door behind her. He slapped the paper down on his lap, angered once again by the fact that she had refused him. He waited for the flush of the toilet and then readjusted himself in the chair stiffly. She came into the living room wearing her green bathrobe, her hair a mess, passed him and went into the kitchen. He heard her fixing herself a cup of the coffee he had heated. He waited for her to come back into the living room, but she did not come. He could picture her, leaning against the counter, surrounded by dirty dishes, garbage, and grease-stained walls, sourly drinking from her cup. She was avoiding him.

"Thalia," he said. After a moment, she moved into sight, her coffee mug held in both hands. She looked sullen rather than sleepy.

"Maybe you'd better sit down," he said.

"What for?"

"I think we have to talk."

"What about?"

Plover held in the smart retort, sighed and said, "About this morning. What was that all about?"

She looked as if she was going to try to pretend she did not know what he was talking about, but then suddenly she changed; her shoulders dropped slightly and her chin came up as she moved toward the couch opposite him and sat on the edge of it, cupping her mug in both hands and looking right into his eyes.

"You're not going to like it," she said. Her voice began normally but rose as she spoke as if she felt some powerful emotion. Plover immediately began to feel frightened.

"What do you mean?" he asked.

"I don't think you want to know," she said. She looked strained, and suddenly Plover wanted very much for this conversation not to have been begun. But he had started it and he was going to finish it.

"I want to know," he said. "You have to tell me."

"All right," she said. He waited for her to go on, but she didn't. She just sat looking at him.

"Go ahead," he said.

"I want to end the marriage," she said.

2

Plover wanted to be reasonable about it. He felt almost relieved, although he did not know why, and he looked at his wife for a long time, while birds sang outside and the morning sun made the white living-room drapes glow hotly behind her. She looked nervous and tense and sad, and for some reason also rather beautiful now. If this went through, they would never make love again. Plover felt a pang, and then realized that it was the first thing he had felt since she had spoken. He reached up to touch his face, watching his wife's eyes follow his hand up to his cheek.

"I can't help it," she said.

"Can't help what?" he asked. Something was wrong with his ears; he could hardly hear himself speak. Then, without waiting for an answer he jumped up and went into the kitchen and drained the last of the bitter day-old coffee into his mug, not bothering to add cream or sugar. He walked almost jauntily back into the living room and sat down, curling his feet under his body. Every action seemed distinct and somehow charged with significance. He smiled at her, his cheeks waxen, but she did not smile back. She seemed to be ready to cry, although it looked to him as if she were going to cry with determination rather than sadness, and much later, months later, he began to understand the strength it had taken, the courage, for her to do this thing. But now he only saw that she was strained and determined and that he, against all expectations, was not happy.

The silence grew longer. Cats wandered into the room, and once Plover jumped up to let one of the cats out the front door. He stood holding the screen open, watching the cat curl up on a hot patch of concrete in the patio, and then left the front door open. When he sat down again he said, as casually as he could, "What's the reason? I think I'm entitled to that, aren't I?"

This is what had taken her so long to speak, Plover learned as he sat with frozen skin listening to her broken phrases and half-finished sentences. It had always irritated him that she would begin a sentence and then stop in the middle of it to think out the end; and he often would finish the sentences for her; but now of course he could not, not only because of the situation, but because he did not understand what she was talking about.

"I don't know how to say this," she said.

"Just say it right out." Plover tried to keep the edge from his voice, but he could not.

15

"I'm not even sure it's true," she said. Plover waited. "It's just that . . ." And she trailed off, looking at the floor.

"I know it sounds corny," Plover said, "but is it something I've done? Or just everything about me?" He laughed nervously. He could feel himself taking over the conversation, and could feel Thalia letting him do it. It was just like her. She would sit there and let him tell her why she wanted to end the marriage.

"This is impossible!" Plover said loudly.

Thalia looked right at him, her head canted to one side, and said very quickly, "I don't love you. I haven't loved you for years. Maybe I never loved you. Maybe I've been fooling myself all these years. But I *don't* love you!" She jumped up and ran into the bathroom. Plover could hear her blowing her nose.

He waited for her to come out. When she did, with Kleenex wadded in her hand, he said, "Okay, more corn. Is there some other guy?"

"No," she said. "It's nothing like that. I told you."

"You told me you didn't love me," Plover corrected. "You didn't tell me *why!*"

She was crying again. "I don't know why, I only know I don't love you and I can't stand to live with you! I'm going crazy!"

Plover said, "Well, of course I don't want to live here if you don't want me," half-expecting her to say, oh, it's not that, but she just nodded as if she understood his feelings, and he began to realize that he was being asked to leave his home. Very faintly (much stronger later) he felt a twinge of something, perhaps outrage, at being asked to leave not for anything he had done, but because his wife

16

had simply fallen out of love with him. She's the one who has changed; she should be the one to leave. He thought of saying this to her, but then the strongest emotion he had felt all morning surged into his chest as he feared that she *would* leave if he did not. No. It would be better for him to go, leaving her with the house and the things and the children. For a moment he could not think, and he shook his head to clear it. The children were at his parents' house in Berkeley. Plover and his wife were supposed to drive over to Berkeley this afternoon, have dinner with his parents and then bring the children home. School tomorrow. They would have to do it. They would have somehow to put things together and go over there and face out his parents, blandly lying, sit through the meal, and then come home. After the children were settled in bed he could leave. This was all going on in his mind as Thalia sat looking at the rug silently, her eyes reddened and a pale blue Kleenex wadded in her hand.

"When do we tell the children?" he said, and the words barely made it out of his mouth before he started crying. The pressure in his head was enormous. He bent forward and put his hands over his eyes, but it was no use. He began to bellow in anguish. His body shook and he rocked forward and back, trying to stop the crying. But he could not. In the part of his mind that was still calm he expected Thalia, on seeing him like this, to come over to him and put her arms around him and comfort him. That was the kind of woman she really was, he realized, and at the same time he knew that she was not going to do it. After a while the sobbing stopped and he went into the bathroom and washed his face with cold water. When he came out he said in a husky voice,

"Sorry. I didn't mean to cry. We have to decide what to tell the children."

"Yes," she said, and she started crying again and had to go into the bathroom. Almost calmly Plover thought how comical it was, the two of them taking turns breaking up, trying to be modern and thinking only of the children. It was a joke. Their marriage had been perfect—so many had told them—and now of course their breakup must be perfect as well. The children first, of course, and then Thalia, she must be taken care of, and then at last and finally, Plover himself, wandering alone, a tragic figure but loveable, because of the great way he handled the divorce, letting her keep *everything* for the children's sake. . . . When she came back he smiled at her and she smiled back.

"You know," he said, "I never thought this would happen to us," and suddenly he was crying again. "God*damn* it!" He sobbed and ran into the bathroom.

3

They settled the matter of the children sensibly. Thalia called his mother and told her that there was trouble, serious trouble, and that the children would have to spend one more night in Berkeley. Plover would be gone when the children came home. Plover did not believe he could move out with the children there. Thinking about it made him cry. But he could sneak out before they got home, and then Thalia could prepare them. It was her job to prepare them because the breakup was her idea. She would have to do all the difficult things. He felt almost vengeful about it.

"Listen, you say you don't love me," he said. "You say you haven't loved me for a long time. Is that enough to throw me out for? There were times I didn't think I loved you, but I didn't move out, for Christ's sake."

"I don't know," she said. "I just know I can't stand it anymore."

"Can't stand what?"

"The way we live. I don't know. Everything. I feel so awful all the time."

"Do you blame me for this? Does it have to be my fault?"

"I don't know. I've thought about it for a long time. I know how hard it is for you to believe me . . ."

"It's not difficult at all," Plover said sharply. He was about to explain to her how it was she felt when he understood at last what she meant. He put his hand over his mouth to stop the words from coming out. There was a silence. Thalia sat with her shoulders hunched together defensively and he sat with his hand over his mouth. After a while he went into the bedroom and dressed.

It was a mess. Clothes all over the closet floor and the chairs, rolls of dust coming out from under the bed. Plover put on his favorite old pair of Levis and a dark blue sweater. The closet bulged with her clothes. His were squeezed over into one corner of one side of the closet. He only owned a few clothes. She had, in addition to what he could see, two bureaus full and two other closets full. Plover could empty his two bureau drawers into a suitcase, pick his clothes out of the closet, hangers and all, and be gone in a matter of minutes. Instead, he went back into the living room. Thalia had not moved. She did not look up at him when he entered.

"Thalia," he said.

After a moment, she looked up.

"I love you," he said.

"I know," she said.

"Doesn't it mean anything to you?"

She started to cry again. He sat down and waited for her to stop. She did not cry the way he did; she sat shaking silently, holding a Kleenex to her nose and letting her eyes run. While she was crying, the German shepherd next door began to bark. The dog was tied to a short chain and never let free because the neighbors' first German shepherd had run out into the street and been killed. The dog was insane, Plover was sure, because he would bark meaninglessly for hours, foam on his mouth and nothing in his eyes. The sound drove Plover crazy, and many times he had wanted to run next door and beg the people to either let the dog go, kill it, or sell it; anything but keep it locked up day and night.

"All right," he said. "Then I'll leave now, just take a few things with me. You'll go get the children in the morning and explain to them why I'm not here. You make it clear to them that this is not my idea at all."

"Yes," she said. "I will."

"Then I'll come back tomorrow and talk to them myself."

"Where will you go?" she asked.

Plover had not actually thought of that. The radio station where he worked was a converted house and had a spare bedroom upstairs that he knew he could use, but the thought of staying there was somehow frightening. He could see himself all alone in the building late at night, sorrowing and moping. It terrified him now suddenly to think of being alone, and the irony of this was that he so often in their married life hungered to be alone. He knew that if he was to make an exit from this house that was to have any style to it, he would have to leave soon and have some place to go. A hotel or motel was out because he could not stand being alone (now that he thought of it), and so he would have to go to the radio station if only to have a telephone handy and have a place to leave his things.

But Thalia said, "What about Tony? Could you stay with him?"

Tony Johns had come and stayed with Plover when *his* wife had thrown him out. By coincidence Thalia had been off with the children visiting her sister. Plover felt a gush of relief at the thought that Tony could not turn him down and would even be a sympathetic ear for Plover's troubles, so sympathetic, in fact, that he might not even ask Plover to talk. It would be enough to know Thalia had thrown him out.

"Yes," he said to her. "Tony, if I can find him. But I'll take my things to the station."

There did not seem to be anything more to say. Thalia was waiting for him to leave.

He packed his things away into the older of their two Volkswagens, on the theory that the children (and therefore Thalia) should have the benefit and safety of the newer car. Then he went back into the house and started a long and strange conversation with Thalia about money and the divorce, if any; and they decided that she should continue to handle the finances and that the divorce, if any, could be instituted in six months. This had been Plover's idea, and Thalia went along with it, and so immediately Plover began thinking in terms of a six-month trial separation. This made him feel better.

4

The parking lot of the radio station was behind the building, dusty gravel surrounded by a high dusty hedge. Plover drove in and parked at his usual place even though there were no other cars in the lot and none expected. Station KLA did not broadcast on Sundays. Plover had control of himself now although he was sure his eyes were puffy and anyone who saw him would know he had been crying. He unlocked the back door of the studio and wedged it open with the little rubber doorstop. The air inside the corridor smelled stale, and Plover walked through to the front office and turned on the air conditioner. Looking out through the front window he could see the bay dotted with sailboats and, beyond them, the abandoned drydocks, on which someone had

nailed a gigantic painted wooden daisy and the word
LOVE. On Bridgeway the traffic was thick and slow.
Plover adjusted the blinds so that he would not have to
look at the view. He sat down for a moment behind Fiedler's desk and looked at the telephone, wondering if he
should call anybody. He wanted very much to have a cigarette, but he had quit and he was not going to start
again. The image of himself sucking on a cigarette while
everyone looked on pityingly disgusted him. Especially
Thalia. See what you've made me do? Whining, cring-
ing, smoking. He smiled bitterly. After he had first quit
smoking he had been a nervous wreck, of course, like
anybody. But he had also had an unusually foul temper,
and everyone had commented on it. Perhaps quitting
smoking had contributed to the breakup. Maybe Thalia
just could not stand it anymore. He felt a rush of sadness,
and to keep himself from crying he jumped up and went
to get his things out of the car. He was very glad for the
hedge around the parking lot.

The third-floor attic bedroom had a slanted roof and
gabled windows on four sides. It was full of dust and
boxes of records. The bed in the corner was simply an
inner springs and mattress on the floor with a Madras
bedspread over it. The attic was not air-conditioned, and
so it was hot and stuffy, even after Plover unstuck two of
the windows and propped them open with sticks. Plover
hung his clothes on the closet rod stretched across one of
the gables. For bedding he had brought his old sleeping
bag and a pillow they had stopped using because it had
begun to leak feathers. He put these on the bed. The two
suitcases he placed on the floor without bothering to open
them, and then he went back downstairs into the now

cool and pleasant offices. He sat down again at Fiedler's desk. Among the pens, pencils, letters, ashtrays, and other junk on top of the desk was a little toy from India, a brass cobra, erect, with its hood extended. A brass point on top of the cobra's head supported a brass rod which had a seated brass bear at either end, the rod curving slightly so that the bears, when the thing was set into motion, appeared to be dancing around the cobra. You set it in motion by giving one of the bears a little push with your finger. If you pushed too hard the rod slipped off the point on the cobra's head. It took real skill to get the bears dancing rapidly around the cobra. Fiedler would sit twirling the bears while he talked on the telephone. Plover liked to play with the thing himself, and he reached out now and poked one of the bears. As he did so the telephone rang, and his hand jerked, knocking the bears off the cobra. Immediately he knew it was Thalia on the telephone. It could not be anybody else. The telephone did not ring on Sundays. He used to come down here often for privacy on the weekends, and the telephone did not ring except for the times Thalia called him. So it was Thalia, calling tearfully to beg him to return home. His chest felt as if his heart had frozen as he lifted the receiver and said a cautious hello.

Thalia said, "Are you all right?"

"Yes," he said.

"I called your mother's house and talked to her. She'll keep the children until tomorrow. I'll go over and pick them up around ten." The rest of the conversation was the same. She had not repented, he was not going to get to come home. He listened to her, spoke to her, and eventually it was all over and he could hang up.

The traffic was still thick, so Plover walked the short mile down Bridgeway to the Old Town Saloon. For most of the way, once past the gas station, the sidewalk was crowded with people and dogs. Most of the people appeared to be tourists even though it was not the tourist season in Sausalito yet. But every Sunday they would come from Plover did not know where (surely these people did not live in San Francisco) to walk up and down Bridgeway in their fat Bermuda shorts and shining see-through shirts, their matched pants suits, gaudy miniskirts, thick legs, weak chins, and sharp suspicious eyes. They were always eating something, too, and always slapping their children, whose faces were greasy or filthy with chocolate. The degenerates of middle America, Plover often thought. He meant degenerate in the sense of physical and moral decay, rather than sexual adventurousness. These were not the fine physical specimens that they should have been after all that wonderful American food and drink. They had bad eyes, bad skin, bent bones, swollen guts, raw voices, bad taste, worse politics, and, Plover begrudged them, most of the money. The hippies and street people along Bridgeway, and there were plenty of them, on the contrary were usually excellent physical specimens, with clear eyes and ruddy skin. They were often dirty, but underneath the dirt they were beautiful people, hard and muscular, sexually active and sexually desirable. In Plover's opinion they were going to magically turn into their parents one of these days, and a more richly deserved fate he could not think of. Plover hated to have them ask him for spare change, particularly since he always had some and never gave any away. Today, however, Plover was wrapped up in his own problems and did not give much thought to the people he weaved in and out among. Practiced walkers in Sausalito, like Plover, kept one eye on the sidewalk; dog shit was nearly everywhere, and also spilled fish-and-chips, burritos, ice cream, and the indescribable muck the tourists and hippies brought with them to eat. You really had to pick your way down the street, and at night it was even worse, because added to the rest of it were the puddles of vomit. But then early in the morning the Sausalito street cleaners would come along with their high-powered water truck and wash it all away. On Monday morning the main street of Sausalito was as clean and sparkling as a travel poster.

5

Plover walked in through the open front door of the Old Town Saloon. He still did not feel hungry but he knew he should eat before he started drinking. He hesitated in the doorway, wondering where he could get something to eat. Eating in public was difficult for him and eating alone in public was almost impossible. He did not know why, he was just terribly self-conscious about eating. He preferred most of all to eat his meals comfortably in front of the television set, watching an old movie. It occurred to him, as he teetered in the doorway of the bar, that his almost new color television set, with its cable receiving twelve channels, was no longer his to watch. For an instant he was afraid he was going to burst out crying right in the bar. Quickly he walked through the place, nodding to a couple of people. When he got to the men's room it was locked, so he went into the women's room and locked the door behind himself. But it was all right, the walk through the bar had cut the emotion. He pissed, washed his hands, and came back out. The tiny dark corridor was crowded with men and women. He smiled at them and made his way into the open bar. Tony Johns was working at the service bar. The stool next to it was open, so Plover sat down.

The place was filled with Sunday sailors in denim jackets, tourists, and a scattering of regulars and chess players. Tony Johns was kept busy filling orders for the two cocktail waitresses. He saw Plover sit down and nodded to him, but the other bartender took Plover's order for a cup of coffee. Plover drank the coffee slowly from its stem glass, turned slightly sideways so that he could see the front entrance. At that time of the afternoon the light from outside came in through both the tall door and the window at the front of the building, creating a glare in the bar, so that people entering appeared in a nimbus of light, unrecognizable shadows until they were all the way into the room. More than once Plover saw Thalia come in to get him, but it was never she, of course, and he did not expect it to be. She was not that kind of person. Once she made up her mind to something, that was it.

Plover felt a touch on his hand. He turned to see Tony Johns leaning across the bar, a look of concern on his narrow face.

"What's the matter?" Tony said.

Plover tried to grin but he could feel his face going out of control, making a wild grimace, a caricature of a smile, and to wipe it off he desperately rubbed his mouth.

29

The funny thing was, he knew just exactly how he looked, because some months ago he had seen Tony do the same thing, at the other end of the bar one night, when Tony had leaned over and said, "Cappie left me," and then tried hopelessly to smile. So Plover waited a moment and said, "Me, too."

Tony blinked, and then one of the girls came up with a large order and he went to work making Ramos fizzes, his eyes flashing over toward Plover every once in a while. When he finished that order there was another one from the other girl, and he filled that, and then there was a pause in the work. He quickly lit a cigarette and went to the other end of the bar, kneeling down to change the record. He came back toward Plover, his cigarette in his mouth, his normally bright eyes lidded with thought. He stopped in front of Plover, not meeting his eyes, and then reached out and patted Plover's hand.

"I get off at seven. You'll stay at my place, of course," he said.

"I was hoping," Plover said.

He spent the afternoon quietly, alternating Calso and coffee, waiting for Tony Johns to get off work. He was not bothered much. At one point, shortly after six, three regulars, all reporters for the San Francisco *Chronicle*, came in from a day at Stinson Beach, sunburned and drunk, and stood next to Plover noisily playing liar's dice, but when he did not join them as usual they gradually turned so that they were a closed group, and Plover gratefully went back to staring at the back bar. Fortunately, from where he was sitting he did not get a reflection of himself.

It was almost too noisy to think, with the dice cups, the loud music, and the increasingly loud chatter and laughter. Plover was not used to sitting in bars without drinking, and the noise was beginning to get to him by the time Tony's replacement arrived.

They walked out through the crowded aisle and onto the street. It was dark and chilly, and most of the tourists and street people had gone home. Tony stood with his hands jammed in his Levi pockets, a thick sweater on over his white shirt. He grinned, showing his bright teeth, and said, "Let's go to the Seven Seas for dinner." Plover nodded, new to this game of deciding where to eat, and they walked silently, side by side, down Bridgeway.

Cappie Johns did not exactly leave Tony. Plover had heard the surface of the story when Tony had moved in with him, just that the marriage was over and Tony needed a place to stay. Even though they had no children he had done the noble thing and left her with the house and most of the goods. But tonight, as they ate in the warm, crowded seafood restaurant, Tony told Plover a good deal more about what had happened.

They had been married eleven years, but for the past five each had looked elsewhere for sex, and even love. Cappie had joined a computer-dating service and almost right away met a man she wanted. For several weeks, while Tony was working in the bar, this man would be over at Tony's house with Cappie. One day, of course, Tony came home early and discovered the two of them in the living room talking. The man left and Cappie explained what had been going on.

"I wanted to sock her," Tony said, "but what would have been the use? She didn't see anything wrong with what she was doing. We didn't love each other, so what difference did it make? Anyhow, I had a hell of a time

31

swallowing it, but I did. I don't know why. To this day I don't know why. I'm happy now, really, for the first time in years; my own man, doing what the fuck I please. You can't believe it, but you'll come around, too."

"I hope so," Plover said, but he did not mean it. "Is that what happened the night you came over to my place?"

Tony laughed. "No. That was before. The night I came over to your place was the night I decided to be generous, or actually, the night *after* I decided to be generous. I thought, what the hell, she likes the guy, maybe she should have a chance to spend the whole night with him. . . ."

Plover interrupted: "Didn't that *hurt* you?"

For the first time, Tony looked irritated. "Of *course* it hurt. But you do screwy things. Anyhow, I told her she could have her boyfriend overnight, and I went out to Muir Beach and stayed at a friend's house. Next day I went home and he was still there. Misunderstanding. She said she thought I meant he could move in. So there it was."

They finished their dinner and Tony insisted on paying the check, grinning in a strange way. Then Plover remembered that on the night Tony had come to him, he had taken Tony to dinner here and insisted on paying the check.

"Let's go for a walk," Tony said. They went south and walked along the breakwater, looking at the lights of San Francisco across the bay. Neither spoke. They walked past the Glad Hand and the Trident and kept walking. Plover wondered if Tony was trying to tire him so that he wouldn't have trouble sleeping later. He was worried about it himself. When he would finally be bedded down for the night at Tony's new place, alone with his thoughts, alone with the image of Thalia. He could feel the panic inside himself reaching for his throat. Abruptly he stopped walking and waited for the feeling to pass. Tony stopped and waited for him, not speaking, his face invisible in the darkness. I'm making an asshole of myself, Plover thought. But no. He's been through it. He knows how I feel.

It was comforting to realize that Tony understood, but not comforting enough to stop the pain. After a while he started walking again, again sensing that this emotion could come along any time it wanted to and knock him down.

They went back to the Old Town Saloon and began drinking, standing at the curve of the bar. Tony drank gin over ice and Plover drank his usual beer. After a while he felt pretty good, and a little while later he felt very good, and when he was in this mood Tony suggested that they leave.

"I understand," Plover said. "You got me drunk so I could sleep. Isn't that right?"

"If you say so," Tony said. They drove in Tony's car over to the station. Then Plover, in his own car, followed Tony to Gate Five. After they got aboard Tony's houseboat, Tony rigged up the couch as a bed and then climbed up into his own sleeping loft and shut off the light. Plover sat in a wicker chair, looking out at the other houseboats and the bay beyond. Faintly he could hear some rock music coming from one of the other boats. He could hear Tony shifting in bed up in the loft. After a long time, he heard Tony say, very clearly, not as if he had been asleep at all. "Hey, you want some grass? It cuts the pain."

"No, thank you," Plover said. He did not want to cut the pain. He wanted to feel it. He was thirty-eight-years-old and his life was destroyed. The pain was the only thing that made him know he was alive.

6

Plover did not even pretend to understand why Thalia
wanted to end their marriage. Of course he had been
foul-tempered for the past few months, ever since he quit
smoking, but he did not think she would throw away
fourteen years for so trivial a reason. And he did not believe her when she said she did not love him. That was
just some female nonsense. Of course she loved him. She
had to love him. In fact, she loved him more than he
loved her. In every relationship there had to be a lover
and a beloved, and in their relationship Plover was the
beloved. He did believe her when she said there was no
one else. If there had been someone else, he would have
known about it.

What kept haunting Plover was an old James Thurber

cartoon. The woman has her hands to her head, and the man says, "With you I've known contentment, Martha, and now you say you're going out of your mind."

Perhaps Plover had slowly bored Thalia to distraction.

No, he thought. I have to stop thinking about it from my point of view and start thinking from her point of view. She is raised on a farm north of Orinda. She and her brothers and sisters do all the chores, milk the cows, weed the truck garden, do the dishes, make the beds, and go to school, while their parents work in the Vallejo ship- yards. Even with the high wages there is never enough money. Thalia baby-sits for extra money, because she is saving up for college. Thalia has ambitions. She wants to be a teacher. (When Plover first hears these ambitions he is amused: teaching is something for a girl to fall back on if she doesn't find a man.)

Thalia finally breaks away from her family at eight- een, moves to San Francisco, and gets a job with a law firm. Most of her work consists of returning law books to their shelves and fetching coffee and snacks for the law- yers. At night she goes to San Francisco State College, downtown. She has virtually no social life.

By the time Plover meets her, in 1955, she is twenty- two and about to graduate from the new campus of San Francisco State. He has just gotten out of the air force and has enrolled to finish up his last two years. He has been a radio announcer for the Far East Network just outside Tokyo, and so he changes his major from English to broadcasting and television, and Thalia is the secre- tary for the chairman of his new department. She has fresh skin, clear blue eyes, and a beautiful smile. She has beautiful laughter. Plover jokes with her and hears the laughter. It occurs to him that he might be able to fuck her.

Two weeks later, parked in a lot overlooking Lake Merced, Plover asks her to marry him. She explains about her ambitions. Plover explains to her about *his* ambitions, to open his own radio station in San Francisco. There is room in the radio station for Thalia, as receptionist, credit manager, personnel manager, and secretary. Perhaps later on she can have her own program. Plover has not yet taken Thalia to bed. This does not happen until a month later, when she shyly accepts his proposal. They are in his tiny dirty apartment on Green Street, and Plover learns that she is a virgin.

Then what happened? They get married and Thalia keeps working for the department chairman while Plover finishes college. He goes to work in radio, but the idea of opening his own station fades, as Plover gets to know the kind of people who actually own stations. They are not his kind of people. It is easier and more fun to spin records and talk. The money gets better and better, and Plover begins to get known around the Bay Area. Time passes. Children are born. Thalia stays home and minds the children.

All right. It is terribly clear. But it is so corny Plover hesitates to put it into words. But he must: Thalia wants a chance to live before she is too old. That's all there is to it.

And try as he might, Plover cannot see why she should not have the chance.

7

For a week it rained, the clouds hanging low over the bay and the mists rising to meet them in the mornings. Gate Five was cold and wet and surrounded by mud. Everyone wore high rubber boots smeared with yellow and black mud, and it became impossible to park a car within fifty yards of the boardwalks. Small ponds formed in the ruts of the graveled road, and after only a few days of rain mosquito larvae could be seen angling up and down in the cloudy water. The wind was cold off the bay and every houseboat including Tony's leaked. On two succeeding nights the power went off, and so there was no light and no heat except on the few boats with gas heaters, and so for Plover, spending a great deal of time alone on the boat while Tony worked at the bar, it was almost a return to a primitive life. He would sit in the darkness looking out through the big French windows at the dark huddled houseboats and the mists on the bay, or stand beside the windows, wearing a sweater under his windbreaker, and watch the drops of rain make circles on the water. If it was low tide he would watch the rain striking the pale smelly mud, trying to think of nothing, trying to stop the pain he believed was self-pity. He had expected some pain to continue but he had not realized how much there would be, how much deeper into it he could go. The rains seemed to help. He did not think he could stand it if the weather was perfect. There seemed to be something terribly wrong about sadness under blue skies, and he wanted to feel sad.

Although he knew it was hopeless, he had decided to tell nobody at the station about the breakup, but when he arrived at six-thirty Monday morning, thoroughly wet and muddy almost to his knees, Cal Martin the engineer grinned and said, "Didn't you go home last night?" And so over their morning cups of coffee in the booth Plover told him what had happened. Martin grinned again and said, "Welcome to the club," holding his coffee mug up in a toast, and did not seem to feel sorry for Plover at all. Martin, Plover remembered, had been married two or three times. He was a tall, thin, long-toothed and long-haired man of about forty who apparently believed that if all women were held upside down they would be more alike than different.

The coffee as usual sent a wave of enthusiasm through Plover, so that by seven when he went on the air, he was almost his old self. He had worried during the night about being able to make sense, but it was not a problem.

After he read the news they opened the telephone lines and he began his conversations for the day. There were ten lines, represented by ten clear plastic buttons on the console before him. When he opened up only three were glowing, but by the time he finished with the first caller the rest had lit up.

It was a typical Monday morning selection. The first caller was a regular, a woman who sounded as if she was at least eighty. She wanted to know what Plover thought about Spiro T. Agnew, the Vice-President of the United States. She was laying a trap for Plover, he knew, hoping to get him to commit himself one way or another. But Plover was ready for her:

"Actually, he's the most interesting Vice-President I think we've had in a long time; even more interesting than Nixon was when he held the office." He paused, to let this sink in, and then said, "But of course Hitler and Stalin were pretty interesting guys, too. What do you think, Caller?"

In rambling, almost incoherent sentences, she explained her feeling that Agnew was the new Charlemagne. After exactly thirty seconds of this, Plover interrupted with a cheerful, "Thanks!" and pressed the next button in the row. It was a male college student who wanted to know why Plover thought he was such a hip character when in actual fact he was a fink, a sellout, and a defender of pigs. Plover liked this kind of caller even though it always tightened his gut to hear their accusations. But they really stirred up the bulk of his audience, who were middle-aged and older. Plover asked the young voice to explain, please, just who it was Plover had finked on, sold out, or defended. The caller said that Plover had sold out the people by being a part of the pig establishment. "You mean because I work for a living?" Plover said, and pushed the next button in the row. The fans really loved that. Throughout the morning Plover was congratulated for teaching the young man a lesson. His position was that he was a catalyst rather than a commentator; that people called him not to hear his opinions but to have him unleash their own. He believed that the success of his program rested on this fact.

The morning wore on and Plover actually forgot to think about himself until Peggy Lavan came quietly into the studio and pressed his shoulder. He knew she must have heard something somewhere, because she was not a toucher. After he read the news and turned the chair over to her he waited until she had gone through her commercial and started a record. Peggy was wearing a lilac crushed-velvet pants suit and silver beads, and Plover wondered how she had gotten through the morning rain. Her hair was not wet and her shoes were not wet. She could always do things like that. Defy the weather. Jump off the rocks into the ocean and not hit her head on the bottom or get carried off by the riptide. Carry drugs in her purse and never get stopped by the police. She read the commercial in her deep booming voice and then introduced the record, flipped the switch, and turned to Plover. "What's this shit about you and Thalia?" she wanted to know.

"I couldn't tell you in three minutes," he said.

"You took a hike?"

Plover explained that Thalia had thrown him out, and

he saw what he thought was a gleam of approval in Peggy's eyes. The record ended and she went into her pitch. He waved vaguely and left the booth. He did not particularly want to talk to Peggy, and anyway, after his three-hour stint on the air he was always emotionally exhausted, sweating heavily, and irritable. Usually at this time of day he would go home through the morning sunlight, congratulating himself on the fact that while most people were beginning their workday he was ending his and had the rest of the day to play in. At home he would take a long relaxing hot shower, often followed by a sunbath on the patio.

The door to Fiedler's office was open. Plover wondered if Fiedler had heard the news, and so he stepped over to the doorway and waved. Fiedler looked up from his desk, his normally sour expression in place. When he saw that it was Plover his mouth relaxed slightly from its bitter tension and he motioned for Plover to enter. Fiedler was wearing a damp-looking yellow and green Hawaiian shirt with a torn pocket, part of his usual beachcomber costume, which everyone who worked for him assumed he wore in order to look poor. Plover noticed that the dancing bears had been restored to the cobra and were rocking slightly. He sat down on the couch, his hands flat on the fabric at his sides. Fiedler went through the business of unwrapping and lighting a cigar and asked Plover if he would have a cup of coffee. Plover said yes, and so they delayed things some more by the coffee ritual. At last Fiedler said, "Well, you had to go and do it, huh?"

"I didn't do anything," Plover said.

"Well anyway we're all sorry around here and we hope you can patch things up," Fiedler said.

In other words, keep your personal problems to yourself, Plover thought. He stood up. "I stink like a goat," he
said.

"See you tomorrow," Fiedler said.

Plover was glad to get away so easily.

8

Tony's houseboat was chilly and damp when Plover got back. Upstairs at the radio station he had changed clothes and put on his lace-up boots, and now he wished he hadn't, because the boots were caked with mud and he didn't want to wear them into the houseboat. He stood with the door open, the rain slapping his back and beginning to wet the faded carpet inside. Tony, looking like a wild-haired character from Dostoevski, stuck his head over the edge of the sleeping balcony and said, "Didn't you turn on the oven?"

"No." Plover sat down in the open doorway and started unlacing his boots. In pulling them off he got the yellowish smelly mud on his fingers. There was a sewage problem in the houseboat area, and he worried about germs. "Oh, Christ," he muttered.

"Would you please turn on the oven and open the oven door?" Tony said. "I'm not getting out of bed until this place heats up."

Wearing Tony's knee-high rubber boots, Plover left the houseboat and went home through the rain. It was a three-mile drive from the Gate Five parking lot to their house in Mill Valley, and in the time it took Plover to drive it, he had convinced himself that Thalia had by now, faced with the children, changed her mind. His spirits rose, and he began to whistle. This happened to him several times that first week, and even afterward: for no reason, or for some reason too tenuous to later analyze, he would become emotionally convinced that Thalia had changed her mind and was only waiting for him to say something. Then she would fall into his arms, sobbing, and beg to be forgiven. This first time, when he opened his front door and saw the faces of his children, he knew it was not true, and he broke down and began crying in front of them.

Paula was twelve and Pamela ten. Their faces were strained and reddened from crying. They reached out for Plover and he took hold of them both and hugged them to him. He had been deeply afraid that his children would not miss him, that they would not care that he was moving away. He did not know where this feeling came from or why he had suppressed it until now, when he knew, could see on their faces and feel through their arms, that it was not true. Yet the pleasure, if you could call it that, of knowing that his children did love him, was just as quickly buried under the despair of the moment. He was going to have to find words of explanation and he did not know what to say. Finally he pulled away from the girls and said he was going to the bathroom.

After he wiped his eyes and blew his nose he went into the bedroom, where Thalia was sitting on the edge of the bed. "Are you all right?" he asked her.

She turned toward him and then stood up. Automatically, Plover moved back, away from her. She said, "I'm all right. What did you say to them?"

"Nothing, yet. What did you tell them?"

Thalia avoided his eyes. "I told them that I wanted to end our marriage, that I couldn't live with you anymore, and that it wasn't your idea, that you weren't deserting them or anything like that, that you wanted to stay, but we had agreed it would be better if you left. They asked me if this meant we were going to get a divorce and I said that we had put that decision off. I said you would come back today and talk to them. That's about all."

"I don't know what to say," Plover said. "You saw me. I cry at the drop of a hat. For Christ's sake I don't have any control over my emotions at all."

"Did you work this morning?"

"Didn't you listen?"

"I was too busy."

"Yeah I worked. Automatically. But I damn near cried in Fiedler's office. Can you imagine me crying in front of Fiedler?" He turned away from her and went to the door of the living room, opening it. The girls were sitting side-by-side on the couch, obviously waiting for him. They were not crying anymore. "I'll be out in a minute," he said. "I have to talk to your mother." He went back to Thalia. "God damn it, you know what's going to happen.

You're here and I'm gone. They can't help but think I was the deserter. You have to do everything in your power to make goddamn sure they don't get the idea I left them, you hear?"

"Yes," she said. "I know how difficult this is."

"I don't think you do, or you wouldn't have done it. You're wrecking three lives for the sake of one, and I don't think that's fair. I think it's goddamn fucking selfish, is what I think. But this isn't the time to argue," he said, and turned and went into the living room, leaving Thalia standing in the bedroom. He sat on the edge of the coffee table, facing the children. He did not have the faintest idea of what he was going to say.

"Girls," he said, "we all have to help your mother. She's under a terrible strain from all this and she has to take care of you two. So we all have to help her. One of the ways you can help is to not ask her a bunch of questions about the breakup, or ask her, nag at her, to have me come back. We can't do that, you know. Do you understand?"

The girls nodded, and Paula, the twelve-year-old, said, "What do you want us to do?"

This tack was apparently working. The girls weren't so awful-looking anymore. In fact, they looked interested. Plover grinned confidently. "Listen, our big job is to keep your mother from feeling guilty about this. I know she told you it was all her idea and everything, but she was just trying to protect me. The truth is, there's just something, we don't know what, between us that makes it impossible for your mother to be happy with me here. We don't want her to be unhappy. At least not any more unhappy than possible. You know what I mean. So don't bug her with questions, help out with the work around here, be cheerful. After all, you must know lots of kids whose parents are split up or maybe even dead."

Pamela said, "Yes. Cindy in my class. Her father was torn up in a wreck."

Plover gulped and said, "Well, you see then, we're not so bad off, are we?"

By the time he finished talking with the girls they were all three laughing and excited. This was going to be fun, and he was going to find an apartment for himself where they could come over and live with him for days at a time, and they'd all have a lot of fun. It was going to be an adventure. He called out for Thalia and after a bit she came hesitantly into the room. She brightened when she saw how everybody looked, and Plover explained to her what he had been saying, and then the four of them sat down and had a good long serious talk about the whole problem. Plover was amazed at how sophisticated even Pamela was about things like this. He left the house late in the afternoon feeling closer to his family, including Thalia, than he ever had before. He drove back to Sausalito feeling positively pleasant. This thing could work out, after all. With all four of them pulling together, Thalia couldn't help but want him back.

9

Tony's houseboat was simple in design. The end that looked out over the water was the living room, with two large glassed doors that should have led to a deck but didn't. In place of the deck there was a rowboat tethered to the houseboat. The boat was old and brokendown and had an old cushion instead of a seat. The end of the next houseboat's walkway extended a bit beyond Tony's boat, and so it was possible for cats to jump into the rowboat. Plover could not understand why the cats would want to do this, but they did. When it was not raining, cats seemed to generate out of the pilings and houseboats, out from under the boardwalks and down from the roofs. Once, while it was raining, Plover saw a cat swim past. He stood up to watch it, and saw it arrive at the pier down the row, dig its claws into an old blackish piling and climb up to the boardwalk, shake itself and march off, tail up. This amazed Plover. He did not know that cats could swim.

The back part of the houseboat was the kitchen, and above it was the sleeping loft, which was open to the living room. The bathroom was between the kitchen and the living room, and like most houseboat bathrooms, it was elevated above the normal floor level so that the gravity toilet would work better.

Everything was damp and cold to the touch unless the electric heater and the oven were on with the door open, and even then it took time to get the dampness out of the walls, and the dampness came right back when the heat was turned off. Tony would not leave the heat on when nobody was aboard the boat because he was afraid of fires, and so he said he was more than glad to have Plover living with him, if only to have an excuse for leaving the heat on longer each day. And of course Plover was always first up in the morning, and the boat was almost cheerfully warm by the time Tony awakened.

One night during that first week, Plover cooked a hamburger steak for himself and sat down and ate it watching television, but by ten o'clock he was bored. He did not want to watch any more television, but he was afraid if he turned it off he would begin to brood about himself. Finally he decided to go down to the Old Town Saloon and have a few drinks. Tony was behind the bar, and that would help. He had been avoiding the bar because most of his and Thalia's acquaintances came in there from time to time, and he did not want to see any of them, or more accurately, he did not want to be seen and questioned. But by tonight he assumed everyone had heard all about it, and the worst that would happen might be a few pitying looks. He felt he could stand that.

It had not been raining, but it started up shortly after he left the houseboat and was making his way down the main dock. By the time he had unlocked his car and gotten inside it was gusting, and a lot of rain came in through the open car door with him, wetting the steering wheel and the inside of the window. Plover lost his temper and his face got hot, as it always did under stress, and perhaps because of this the inside of the windows fogged up badly. Plover found the old T-shirt he used to wipe the windows with down on the floor on the passenger side, and after he got the engine going and the heater on he began to rub the moisture off the windows, but there was mud all over the T-shirt, and all he did was get the windows dirty. Rummaging through the glove compartment he found a couple of old Kleenexes (Thalia's) and used them to clean the windshield. By this time the heater was putting out and so he could see to drive. He passed several hitchhikers on the way, their white and black faces appearing and disappearing suddenly in the rain. Some of them Plover was afraid to let into the car, and so he let the others go, too. He had hitchhiked as a kid, and he knew what it was like, but it did not make him pick anybody up.

The Old Town Saloon was hot and damp and crowded. Plover pulled open the big door and felt the heat billowing out around him in visible clouds of condensation and tobacco smoke. The music and chatter were loud and exciting, and for the first time in days Plover felt interested in what he was doing. He waved and said hello and smiled at several people as he made his way down the crowded aisle as he had on so many other nights. The place seemed filled with people Plover knew, and if any of them had heard the news about the breakup they didn't show it. Everything was going to be all right. There was a tiny wedge of space next to the service bar, and on the pretext of talking to one of the girls he elbowed his way in, and Tony put down a napkin and a beer, waved off payment, and Plover was at home.

An hour later he was happily playing liar's dice with one of the engineers from the station and a cameraman from KPIX, winning more than he was losing, drunk, or at least feeling high and very good, when he saw Thalia come into the bar in her black raincoat, her hair wet around her abnormally white face. Plover turned away, everything falling apart again. He lifted his beer and drank from it, but he was sober now and would stay sober. He wanted a cigarette but resisted picking up one of the packs on the bar and taking one. The music played loudly and the people made their usual sounds, but now Plover hated it. He was just short of panic. He wanted to run from the place. He wanted to go over to Thalia and slap her face and kick her ass and get her out of there. The bar was his place to go, the last one he had left, and here she was coming in to ruin it for him. He kept his head down and his beer mug in front of him, and when the cameraman asked him if he was ready for another round of dice he forced a grin and said no. The game went on beside him, the slap of the dice cups noisy and infuriating, now that he was not playing. He avoided Tony, but Tony was so busy it did not matter. Five or ten minutes passed, and Thalia did not come over to him, did not touch him on the shoulder and smile hesitantly, so the fantasy that she had come looking for him died and he went back to the original idea that she had come in here to ruin the place for him. She had begun that long before they broke up. He had come down here to get away, to have a few hours' peace and company, and of course he often brought her with him, but she had begun coming in alone, afternoons and sometimes evenings, and even coming in when he was already there. She had taken his home and his children, but she was not going to take his bar. He looked up, angry, to find where she was sitting. He could not see her anywhere. He waited, glowering, for her to come out of the toilet, but she did not. He went up to the front of the bar, as if to telephone, and looked at the tables by the front window. She was not there, either. So she had left. Probably as soon as she saw him.

Plover went back to his beer knowing Thalia had come to Sausalito burning with loneliness and had left when she saw him because she knew what it was doing to him. He felt a deep and powerful shame for the things he had been thinking. But underneath the shame there was also pleasure that Thalia too felt the loneliness. Let her find out what it's like, he thought, when he permitted himself to. He even went further and thought about getting the children away from her, the house, everything, and making her go out into the empty world by herself. That would teach her.

But he knew better. Beneath her gentleness Thalia was tough, far tougher than Plover. Once when they had been living in San Francisco and Plover was making almost nothing as a disk jockey on a classical music station, taking trade-outs in place of salary, there had been a party in their flat. While Plover stood drunk in the bathroom trying to piss he could hear through the bedroom door a young man named Deakle trying to talk Thalia into going to bed with him. Deakle was very large and drunk and had a reputation for erratic behavior. Plover had not invited him to the party and didn't know who had. Thalia's murmur through the door was not loud enough for Plover to be able to hear her exact words, but it sounded as if she was handling Deakle well enough. "But I love you!" Deakle bellowed and left the bedroom. Plover came out, convinced that he would have come running if Deakle had put a hand on Thalia. For the next hour Deakle went around to everybody at the party and explained drunkenly how he loved Thalia and made a pass at her and she had turned him down. Plover did not see what happened next, but Thalia later told him that Deakle had suddenly grabbed her and forced her into the bedroom, and when she swore at him and said, "You're hurting my arm!" Deakle's face twisted with pain and he threw Thalia away from him and dug into his pocket for his little penknife. Thalia watched him fumble the blade out and without looking her in the eye yell, "I'm gonna kill myself!" and with a wild gesture, probably supposed to miss by inches, he instead cut a gash in his wrist, just below his watchband, that must have been an inch deep. Thalia screamed when she saw the blood spurt out, and Deakle's eyes got wide and he collapsed to the floor, flailing his arms and yelling, "Lemme die! Lemme die!"

At the scream Plover and several other people crowded into the bedroom. Plover saw the blood and fought down a sickening lurch in his stomach. He knew the arm would have to have a tourniquet, so he got a necktie from the closet and kneeled beside Deakle, who was still thrashing and yelling and bleeding. He tied the necktie around Deakle's arm, but it didn't seem to have any effect on the bleeding. Then Thalia was on her knees beside him, a towel in her hand. Plover moved back as Thalia untied the necktie and placed it differently, then tied it tighter. The bleeding slowed. Thalia wrapped the towel around the wrist and tore it and tied it almost professionally.

"Lemme die!" Deakle moaned. He began to thrash again, now that his arm was bandaged. He kept his eyes shut.

"Help him to his feet," Thalia said, and a couple of the men got Deakle up. "There's been a lot of noise, we have to get him out of here to a hospital before the police come," she said.

Deakle let the two men lead him toward the front door, but then in the middle of the living room he looked around and saw everyone watching him, and perhaps from shame or embarrassment he tore himself away from the men and dropped to the rug. "Lemme die!" he yelled.

Thalia got to her knees beside him and leaned down close to his face. "Look at me," she said. Deakle stopped thrashing and looked up at her. "Nobody's going to let you die," she said. Her voice was low and calm. "Either you'll go to the emergency hospital and get your wrist fixed and then go home, or you'll stay here until the police come. If you wait for the police, they'll take you not to the emergency hospital but to the county hospital, where they'll fix your wrist and then lock you in the mental ward. They'll keep you there thirty days, and if you can't prove you're sane, they'll send you to Napa. Would you like that?"

Deakle shambled off to the hospital and they never saw him again, although Plover received a new necktie in the mail, a replacement for the one Deakle had carried out on his arm. After it was all over and a small group were sitting around drinking wine, no longer expecting the police, someone asked Thalia, "Where'd you hear about that mental hospital routine?" and she laughed, her blue eyes merry, and said, "Oh, I just made that up to get him out of here!"

She was tough. Maybe all women were tougher than men, Plover thought over his beer. Maybe they have to be. The crowd was thinning out and it did not seem to be raining anymore. Plover had one last beer sitting at the bar and then said good night. He thought Tony looked as if he wanted to say something and so he paused for a moment, fearful that Tony wanted to talk about Thalia's earlier entrance and exit, but Tony just said, "Sleep tight," and Plover grinned and left.

He had hoped that all that beer would make it easier for him to get to sleep, but he was barely dozing when he felt the boat shudder, as it always did when somebody stepped aboard, and then heard the low laughter of a woman. He heard the door open and Tony go, "Shh. No lights," in a whisper, and then say, "Frank?"

Plover did not answer. It would be better to pretend to be asleep.

Tony chuckled and said in a low voice, "Mollie, this is the famous Franklin Plover. Frank, Mollie."

"Oh for God sake, you must be kidding," a woman's

voice said. Then she laughed again. Plover thought she had a beautiful laugh. He was trying to think of who she could be. He did not know any Mollies who came into the bar.

"Since the couch is taken, I guess we'll have to do our drinking upstairs," Tony said. Mollie giggled, and Plover could hear Tony getting his bottle of Scotch and a couple of glasses. "No ice," he said, almost in tune with Plover's thoughts. "That's okay," Mollie said. It took the two of them a long time to get up the ladder to the sleeping loft, and it seemed to Plover as if Tony was pretending to be as drunk as Mollie. They giggled and murmured and finally got up to the top, and Plover tensed himself against hearing the sounds of their lovemaking. There had been a time when he would have thought secretly listening to others making love would have been exciting, but now it only would serve to remind him of Thalia and that would make him sad. He thought viciously of waking up and making it impossible for them. But what actually happened was that, as their sounds grew less and less, he dozed off. He awakened briefly once when Mollie cried and swore her way through an orgasm, but he drifted right back to sleep, as if it did not concern him at all.

10

When Plover's alarm went off he reached out quickly to throw the switch. It was a tinny little German eight-day clock Plover had bought in a Sausalito drugstore the Monday after his breakup, and he was still not used to it. For one thing, it ticked. For another, it rang instead of awakening him to music. This morning he had already been awake when the alarm went off, waiting for it with the sleeping bag pulled up to his chin, looking out at the pale blue morning sky. There were no clouds, for the first time in days, and the bay was a mirror, reflecting the dark outlines of the houseboats and boardwalk. The woman upstairs with Tony moaned and readjusted herself in bed. Plover waited a moment, and then slowly unzipped his bag and got up.

He turned on the oven first and then dressed quietly in the semilight. He would have his morning coffee at the station, because he did not want to be in the houseboat when Tony and the girl awakened. But as he was leaving the bathroom he could see her bare legs coming down the ladder. She had thick meaty legs and her underpants hung on her as if they were two sizes too large. Above the pants she was wearing one of Tony's faded red sweatshirts. Her face was puffy with sleep and her hair frizzy. Plover recognized her. She came in the bar often and sat in the front, reading. Because she was so hefty and phlegmatic-looking, Plover had never paid any attention to her. Now they looked at each other, and Mollie smiled and said, "Where's the pottie?" Plover gestured with his thumb and moved out of the way. She smelled faintly of perfume and sweat as she brushed past him, and he had a sudden vision of himself following her into the bathroom and raping her. He smiled and began to make coffee.

When she came out of the bathroom she said, "Jesus, my head is killing me." She stood in front of the oven hugging her breasts and yawned without covering her mouth. Plover noticed that several of her back teeth were missing on the right-hand side. "Scuse," she said. "Do you have any aspirin?"

"I don't know," Plover said. He went into the bathroom and looked in the cupboard. He could not find anything, but looking through the kitchen cabinets he came across aspirin, vitamins, and a brown bottle full of different size and color pills. "Yum yum," Mollie said. She opened the brown bottle. "I wonder what these little goodies are."

"You shouldn't take those if you don't know what they are," Plover said.

"Aw, bullshit," Mollie said. "I couldn't feel any worse than I do now, could I?" She selected two or three of the pills and washed them down with a glass of water. Plover reminded her that she had wanted aspirin and she thanked him and took four aspirin. Plover wanted to tell her that the recommended dosage was two tablets, but he didn't. She made him nervous. He did not like the way she talked and he did not like her looks. Her skin was pale and unhealthy and her features were blunt. She had small eyes and looked to Plover like a peasant. She excited him sexually, but he reasoned that any woman under the same circumstances would do the same. She appeared to be about thirty years old. Plover wondered why Tony had brought her home with him, and then sneered inwardly at himself for wondering.

Mollie said, "Well, back to the rack," and went up the ladder again, while Plover watched her ass. He hoped she would not waken Tony and start making love to him. He did not want to listen, and the coffee was almost ready. But she did not, and he drank his coffee, looking out at the beginnings of a perfect day, and wondered where in hell he was going to live. He certainly could not stay at Tony's any longer. He did not like the idea of women coming in. It was great for Tony (with certain esthetic reservations) but it was hell for Plover, who did not want to be reminded that sex or love existed; at least not yet. So he would have to move out. He would, anyway. He could not stay with Tony forever. Tony had only lived at his house for four days. This was Friday, so he had already been here five days.

What he really had to do was admit that Thalia was not going to let him come home. So he had to find a place to live. Just thinking about it made him go through the same old emotions that had been riding him all week. He stood up and said, "Shit!" and stamped off to work.

11

There was nothing to do in the rain most of the time. Plover had been congratulating himself on the fact that he only had to work three hours a day, but now he wished he had something compelling, like a job, to keep him from sitting around thinking about himself. He was not due to see the children again until the weekend, and he wanted to leave Thalia alone so that she could have time to think. Tony, of course, had a life of his own to live, and Plover was surprised to look around and see that he actually had no friends, just acquaintances. Tony was obliged to put up with him, but nobody else was. Nobody whose shoulder he could really cry on, no girls who would murmur with sympathy and take him into their beds. In fact, the only bright spot he could find was that he had not taken up smoking again.

All of his possessions, his books and records, his paintings, drawings, photographs, toys, movie cameras, rugs, favorite chairs; his cats and his goldfish, his shower stall, the very smell of his house; his patio, with its own seasonal smells; everything that was the context of his life had been stripped from him, and it made him feel naked and lost. It was not the same as if he were on a trip. When you are on a trip you know that your things, your life, still wait for you. This was a different feeling, and the only thing Plover could think of to compare it to was free-fall in space. You are falling, but you do not experience the sensation of falling. You *know* you are falling, alone, in the emptiness of space.

One morning he came in from work to find Tony making breakfast. Plover had, of course, heated the place up before he had left earlier. Tony turned toward him and started to ask him if he wanted anything to eat, when he broke off and said, "Hey, man, you look terrible. Are you all right?"

Plover had not been feeling particularly bad at the moment, but he said, "Well, you know . . ."

Tony went into the tiny bathroom and came out with a little green vial. "Take one of these, why don't you." He shook a couple of small blackish pills onto his palm and held them out to Plover.

"What are they?"

"Tranquilizers," Tony said. "They're very mild. The mildest they make."

Tranquility seemed like an impossible dream to

Plover, but he took one of the pills and swallowed it with a glass of milk. He sat at the kitchen table talking to Tony while he waited for the pill to take effect, and then because he was feeling sleepy he lay down on the couch. He slept for eighteen hours.

As he waited in the darkness of early morning for time to go to work, he told himself that he should have known he could not take tranquilizers. Even antihistamines put him to sleep. Of course it would be fine if he could take a pill that would make eighteen hours vanish; that would solve the problem of how to get through each day. Plover could see how people could become drug addicts; nearly anything was better than this feeling of emptiness. He looked at his watch, squinting to make out the radium numerals and hands. It was just a little after five-thirty. A gust of wind rocked the boat, and rain spattered against the windows. Plover felt himself coming apart. There were knives in the kitchen drawer, and the thought terrified him. He put on Tony's rubber boots and his own heavy rain jacket. There were two telephone booths next to the gas station out on the road. He walked out through the mud, his head down and his arms crossed against his chest, and got himself into one of the booths and called his number. After four rings, Thalia answered.

"Honey," he said, and his voice went upward into a squeak, "I can't stand it. You have to save me." The last words were too high-pitched to be understood. He tried to breathe deeply, to stop the sound, but every time he started a sentence the same thing would happen. He was sobbing now, heavily, and in frustration and agony he beat his free hand against the glass wall of the booth.

"Where are you?" Thalia said.

"Can I come over?" he managed to say.

"Yes," she said.

The drive to Mill Valley seemed to calm him down. He parked at the bottom of the driveway and walked up through the now soft rain. The porch light was on, and Thalia answered the door quickly. She was wearing her old robe, but she did not look as if she had been asleep. Plover stepped past her into the house and said, "Hi," lightly.

"Can I get you some coffee?" she asked.

"That would be nice," he said. He sat down, and when she brought him the coffee, in his favorite mug, he said, "I really don't know what the hell I'm doing here."

"Couldn't you sleep?" she asked.

"You know how it is."

"I couldn't sleep, either," she said. "I guess we've been together so long we have the same moods."

"Yeah, the way people's dogs get to look just like them after a few years." He did not like the sound of that after he said it and so, looking down at his coffee, he said, "Thanks for letting me come over. I was pretty rocky there. Just being here makes me feel better."

"I know," she said.

"I was kind of losing my sanity, laying there in the dark. I couldn't take any pills and I couldn't sleep, and my mind kind of kept going out of control."

"I know," she said. "Once, years ago, when I was working, I spent one whole evening while you were at the station holding a knife to my stomach. I was lying on the bed, dressed, just holding the knife. The big butcher knife. I guess it was something like that for you, wasn't it?"

Plover was staring at her. He had never heard this story about the butcher knife before. "What was wrong?" he asked her.

"You mean with the butcher knife? Oh, that was a long time ago. I just felt bad."

She was letting him know that it had happened to her, too, and that she understood, and that she was not asking him for details or explanations, and so he did not ask her to explain further. It was just another of the things they had not gotten together on when they should have. Or maybe it was impossible for two people to be that close. He did not know. His own impulse had passed, and he had to get out of there. They talked about the children for a few minutes, Plover had another cup of coffee, and then he thanked her again, squeezed her arm and left for the station.

He was brilliant that morning, if he had to say so himself. He was funny and sharp, and when called for, compassionate. Even Cal Martin seemed impressed, and Peggy Lavan touched him on the shoulder as she replaced him at the board.

12

As he ended his program, Plover watched Peggy Lavan through the glass. She was talking to Bob Hamilton, and while Plover watched she laughed and reached out to touch Bob on the arm. It was a gesture Plover had seen her make a hundred times, but this morning there was something sensual about it, something that made Plover want her to touch *him* that way. Peggy Lavan. He had never actually thought of her as a girl he might take to bed, perhaps because he was a little bit afraid of her.

She was a dynamic girl, only twenty-two or three and already the only female disk jockey in the Bay Area. That didn't sound like much until you stopped to think that a girl making three hundred dollars a week was a rarity, especially when all she did was murmur into a microphone. But everyone knew Peggy Lavan was not going to be a disk jockey long. She had ambitions and talent as an actress, and she had the drive to make it. A lot of people wondered why she was wasting her time in Sausalito, but they failed to understand, as Plover understood, that Peggy was no fool, and was not going to rush down to Hollywood on a wing and a prayer and hope to land work in a few weeks. Peggy systematically saved one hundred dollars a week of her pay, toward her Hollywood war chest. When she had ten thousand dollars in the bank, she would head south in style.

During the commercials separating their programs, Plover swallowed and said, "Listen, can I meet you after you get off?"

She cocked her head to look up at him and he added, "I have to talk to somebody . . ." and she smiled and said, "Okay, pick me up." She sat down at the console, took off all her rings and flexed her fingers. "Into the breech, cried the six hundred," she said, and threw open her microphone.

Plover decided not to hang around the studio waiting for her. It was not raining, so he walked to downtown Sausalito under the clouds and had breakfast in a hole-in-the-wall and read the morning *Chronicle*. Over a third cup of coffee he examined the Marin County rental want ads. They did not look too promising. But he had always heard that places in Sausalito were passed from friend to friend, and never did appear on the open market. He would have to ask Peggy about it. He smiled to himself, wondering exactly why he was going to meet her. He did not think he would make a pass at her. She would probably laugh at him and say something cutting.

On the other hand, she might make a pass at him. Plover smiled and refolded the paper neatly and returned it to the top of the cigarette machine. He paid his check and said good-bye to the waitress and went out into the cool air. "Make a pass." Jesus. "How about a date, Honey?" Or, "Let's neck!" Plover was going to have to learn somewhere the language of courtship. He was fifteen years out of date.

Well, not really. He had fooled around a little. Not much, just a little. He stopped in front of the Tides and stood looking in the show window at a display of books, his hands in his pockets. How many? The whore in Tiajuana. Patsy, the secretary at KFRC. Eight years ago, and she had gotten drunk at one of those payola parties at a motel on Lombard Street and drunkenly demanded that he take her home. She had definitely been the one to make a pass at him, unzipping his pants and grabbing at his cock while he tried to drive through San Francisco. Come to think of it, he had never actually *balled* her; both that time and the time he had gone over to her apartment drunkenly at three in the morning she had insisted on going down on him.

He wondered what had ever become of Patsy. Little girl with tight blond curls and hysterical eyes. Typical cheer leader over the hill at twenty-five. He started walking down the street again, vaguely nervous because he did not have a destination, trying to remember if there had been any other women in his life since he had been married. Just two? And one of them a whore? No. He had forgotten all about tall Susan. He had been talking on the telephone at Vesuvio's one night when he did not want to go home, and she had come drifting down the

69

stairs from the women's room and he had said, "A vision of loveliness" or something equally corny, but she had smiled and they had gotten into a conversation and he had ended up in her bed, a few blocks away. And then he had never seen her again. A genuine pickup. Very nice, too. Tall and pretty with large warm eyes.

And, as he remembered now, totally frigid and full of excuses. And he had suffered terrible guilt feelings for days, not only because he had betrayed Thalia, but because he was afraid tall Susan had given him the clap.

Suddenly he remembered something he had forgotten since the moment Thalia had told him she wanted to end the marriage: it was not exactly a thought; more of a feeling; and he could not express it in words. A sense of desperation, of feeling that the years were passing and he was missing out on nearly everything. He had not blamed Thalia, but she had been at the root of it. He could now remember driving up the Waldo Grade, on his way home from San Francisco one afternoon, feeling an almost heart-stopping despair. All around him people were whizzing off to surprise encounters, adventures, loves, and hates, while he was chugging uphill in his Volkswagen toward home and deathly boredom. Yes. He had felt that way more than once, many times, many many times.

And yet now that he was free he felt only anguish and misery. Was he fated always to be unhappy? He wondered. Maybe everybody suffers most of the time, and we're all ashamed to admit it to each other.

Plover desperately wanted a cigarette. What the fuck difference did it make, whether he smoked a cigarette or blew his brains out? But just then he saw a very pretty young girl in a miniskirt and a bright yellow short slicker coming toward him. He watched her, and she met his eyes and smiled as she went by. Plover had to laugh at himself. From despair to lust in half a second. The truth was, he felt pretty good this morning, all things considered. And in two hours he would be beginning an adventure of his own, when Peggy Lavan came shyly out into the parking lot and got into his car.

13

They went to the Trident for lunch, but as soon as they
sat down they were joined by two bearded long-haired
men in fatigue jackets, tie-dyed shirts, and leather pants.
Peggy introduced them to Plover as Greek and Johnny.
They smiled at him politely, gave him their limp hands
to shake, and then began murmuring to Peggy. Plover
did not want to overhear the conversation. He was furious that Peggy had let them sit down at all. He spent
most of the time staring at nothing. The Trident was full
of colorful people and loud music, the kind of place
Plover detested. He had brought Peggy here because he
had thought she would like it. But it turned out she knew
nearly everybody in the place. She was, of course, famous, as the hip lady disk jockey. Plover assumed that

none of the Trident crowd got up in time to hear his show. And anyway, his face was not well known. Still, he was furious.

When Peggy's health food milk shake and plate of bulgur and Plover's shrimp salad arrived, Greek and Johnny left.

"What did they want?" Plover asked her.

She laughed. "Weren't you listening? They want me to lend them twenty-five hundred dollars so they can go to Mexico and buy grass. They guaranteed me five thousand."

After a few moments of quiet eating, Plover said, "Well, are you going to do it?"

"Are you kidding? They're probably narks anyway."

During the rest of the meal people came and went, always to talk to Peggy, never to talk to Plover, although they were polite enough, and Plover ate stolidly, wondering again why he was here. Of course it was nice being with a hotshot like Peggy Lavan, but he wanted more from her than reflected glory. He was determined now that he was going to make a pass at her, if only out of revenge.

After lunch they walked down to the Old Town Saloon for a coffee and brandy. The place was nearly empty, and Tony was on duty alone. Plover introduced him to Peggy when he came around the bar with their drinks.

"That's the guy I'm staying with, on his houseboat," Plover said to her after Tony had gone back behind the bar. "He's one of the nicest guys in Sausalito."

"I dig houseboats," Peggy said.

Without looking at her, Plover said, "Would you like to come down and see the place?"

"Maybe later," Peggy said.

"You live alone, don't you?" Plover asked her.

"Not exactly. There's a girl living with me. She pays a quarter of the rent and does the housework. College girl."

"I mean, *essentially*, you live alone. Right?"

"Oh, essentially, yes. You mean I don't live with a man."

"Not exactly. What I mean is, I have to get used to living alone. That's really what I wanted to talk to you about. I don't know a goddamn thing about it. I mean, like, how do you find an apartment? Stuff like that."

"It's like getting to Carnegie Hall," she said. "You have to have practice at it. You look in the papers? Fantastic. But there are a few joints around. I feel like getting drunk this afternoon. Will you buy me another brandy?"

"Sure," Plover said. He finished his and went up to the bar with the pony glasses.

"Getting the lady plastered?" Tony asked.

Plover giggled and winked at him. Tony poured them two very generous shots of brandy and waved his hand when Plover reached for his money.

"Lots of luck," Tony said.

An hour later the bar was filling up, and Plover had exhausted the subject of living alone. He was now certain of one thing: Peggy Lavan was a determined cheapskate. He was just as certain that she had come to lunch with him in order to have a free meal, followed by free brandy, not for any other, more personal reason.

She knew every cheap shortcut in the book. She shopped on sale days armed with newspaper ads and gift coupons. She stole her newspaper. Her fantastic wardrobe she made herself, wore each item a few times, and then sold as new to a select sucker list of rich college girls her size. If no one offered to buy her dinner, she often went without or made a meal of apples and raw nuts. She was not a health food freak, she explained, but some kinds of health food were cheap, and you knew exactly what food value you were getting. If somebody wanted to impress her with a steak dinner at Ondine's, she was willing and eager.

"You're kind of close with a buck," Plover said at one point, more from admiration than anything else.

"You better fucking believe it," she said. "I've been on my own since I was thirteen years old. Nobody's going to take care of me, I learned pretty goddamn fast. So baby learn to take care of baby. When I get in pictures I'm not going to be one of those assholes who pick and choose their pictures so they'll look good to themselves. With me it's money all the way."

"Wouldn't it be easier just to marry money?"

"And have to live with some old bastard with rotten breath? Fuck that noise. Freedom and money, that's my battle cry."

"Baby, I wish you all the luck in the world," Plover said with a grin. "I really think you're gonna make it."

She put her hand on his arm, and he remembered how, that morning, he had wanted her to do just that. But now she was saying, "Plover, you know, you're an odd bastard. I think I like you."

"Didn't you, before?"

"Well sure, but not the same. I never really got to know you. Does anybody? You're not a bad guy, really. How come Thalia dropped you?"

75

Put that bluntly, Plover did not know how to answer the question. "I don't know," he said.

"Do you want to talk about it?"

"Actually, no."

"Thank Christ. I thought that's what this was all about. I thought you wanted to cry on a female shoulder." She leaned toward him and kissed him lightly on the cheek. He could smell her perfume for an instant, and it made him faint with desire. "Let's go see that houseboat," she said in a low voice.

14

When something like this goes wrong, Plover thought later, when he was calm enough to think about it at all, it is best not to try to analyze why, but just let it drift with all the other botcheries of life.

He was not ready, that's all. Just plain not ready. On the surface there was nothing he wanted more than to sleep with Peggy Lavan, but his subconscious (he reasoned) would not let him. First, when they got to the muddy parking lot at Gate Five, Plover pinched her on the arm. He had meant to take her gently by the arm and help her out of the car, but he pinched her instead. She gave him a look and said, "I can manage," and he said, "Okay," and backed off. He got all muddy and she didn't.

Then, on the way out the dock, Plover saw ahead of them a pack of dogs, some lying down, some standing looking in their direction. Plover did not like the dogs of Gate Five, and he especially did not like them in large groups. RADIO PERSONALITY TORN APART BY DOG PACK was a headline that occurred to him more than once.

Most of the dogs seemed to be combination German shepherds and Dobermanns. There were very few small dogs at Gate Five. These big ones belonged to no one, often left behind at the end of summer by travelers, and they foraged for miles around, even eating the vegetables out in back of the Big G supermarket at times. Although he had never heard of anyone being attacked by the dogs, Plover was certain that the day would come when they would all band together, perhaps fifty or sixty of them, and go berserk. They would begin by killing a few cats, and then, blood-simple, they would start in on babies and children, graduating to adults finally, and then the police would come and people would be shot by stray bullets, fires started, and Gate Five would disappear into the bay.

But of course that was fantasy, wasn't it, and all Plover had to do was get by the seven or eight dogs in their path without communicating fear to either the dogs or Peggy. He did not make it. As they approached the dogs he could not help reaching for Peggy's arm (although he was careful not to pinch her again), and then when one of the dogs got to his feet and started toward them, Plover screamed, "Get the fuck out of here, you bastard!" and kicked wildly at the dog. The dog ducked easily and went away. None of the other dogs paid any attention, not even to the scream.

All right, so by the time they got to the houseboat itself Peggy knew that Plover was a frightened little coward. A real sexual fillip for her. He showed her the boat bluntly ("That's the sleeping loft, this is the kitchen,") and sat down on the couch, waiting for her to say, "Well, I have to go."

But instead she sat next to him and said, "You got any dope?"

"No," he lied. He did not know why he lied. His immediate defense was that he did not have any dope, since the marijuana belonged to Tony.

She reached out a finger and touched him on the cheek. He could feel the smooth sharp edge of the nail. She said, looking into his eyes, "Take it easy, man."

That was the time for him to take a deep breath, admit he was shy, and let her take charge. But he could not do that. For one thing, he had to go to the toilet. If they started necking, there would be no time to go to the toilet later, and he did not want to make love in this condition. Women could do it, he had heard, but not men. But instead of getting up and going to the toilet, he started a conversation about astrology.

It was, he knew later, the worst thing he could have decided to talk about. Peggy was a smart girl, but she did have a bug about astrology. Plover hated astrology. He hated to have people ask him his sign, and as a matter of routine, he always lied about it. No one ever noticed. He told this to Peggy and saw the disapproval on her face. He kept talking. He went into the history of astrology, about which he knew very little, and then perhaps just to keep talking, he went into a lecture on the differences between sun time and star time, which, he could see, was not interesting Peggy much. Then he went to the toilet. When he came out he sat a little farther away from her.

"I have to go," she said.

He got up and said, "I'm sorry."

"That's cool," she said. "You want to run me up to the station and my car?"

"Oh, yeah," he said. She was standing. He moved toward her, took her by the arms, and pulled her close to him. He kissed her ear. She seemed to be very rigid. He smelled her hair for a while, and then let her go. He smiled sheepishly, but she did not smile back.

Just as they stepped outside, it began to rain.

"I'm going to get all wet," she said, as if it was Plover's fault.

"I'm sorry," he said.

But at the station she leaned over to him and kissed him on the mouth and said, "Take it easy, man. Things will get better," and then slipped out and ran into the parking lot. So she understood, and it was going to be okay tomorrow morning, when he would have to see her again. Still, he spent the rest of the afternoon embarrassed, and when Tony got home and asked him how he had made out, he only said, "Well, you know."

"Yeah, man," Tony said. "That's some chick."

15

During the next few weeks Plover continued to live with Tony Johns, but now instead of hoping for a reconciliation, he was househunting, or at least he was not supposed to be hoping for a reconciliation and he was supposed to be househunting. Actually, both were difficult for him. Every few days he would talk to Thalia on the telephone, and nearly as often he would beg her permission to come over to the house, if only to see the children. This was a lie, they both knew. He did not much want to see the children. He loved them and he missed them, but Thalia stood in the way. As long, he felt, as there was the slightest hope they might reconcile he needed to pursue her. He hated using the children as an excuse, but there was nothing he could do about it.

The visits were always strained, even though the children seemed to have accepted the whole situation much more easily than Plover had expected (or hoped), and so while Paula and Pamela were always glad to see him, they were not very dramatic about it. After all, he reasoned, they have lives of their own to live. Thalia was not glad to see him, although she tried to be polite and tried to make him comfortable. Each time, as he left, he would move to take her by the arm or put his hands on her hips, hoping to feel her move toward him, and each time she would slide nervously away from his touch and they would part awkwardly, usually with Plover muttering, "G'bye" without looking at her and Thalia remaining silent. After he left the house he would swear he would not do that again, that he would let Thalia have the time and peace she needed to understand what was going on. He reasoned that if they ever were to get together again it would come from his letting her alone to work out her problems, not from his crowding her and always being there. But he would grow lonely or homesick or some excuse would occur to him, and he would call.

Part of his problem, he kept telling himself, was that he had too much free time. He could not read because he could not concentrate. Television bored him sick, although he had watched it regularly enough when he had been living at home. In fact, it had been one of the sore points between himself and Thalia for a long time, and he had not realized it. She said that she could not concentrate on anything with the television blaring away, and he wondered what it was she had to concentrate about. Besides, he resented the fact that she would not watch television with him. She never seemed to want to do anything he did. Anyway, now he could hardly watch the stuff, except late at night, full of Tony's marijuana.

So, in a way, Plover looked forward to househunting. He even had visions of decorating his new place as a way of filling uncounted hours of time, browsing in the junk stores, learning about prices and styles, a faceless but beautiful young woman at his side as they shopped for drapery materials or examined the pottery in little out-of-the-way shops on Clement Street or Polk Street in San Francisco.

He spent one very pleasant sunny morning sitting in an old weatherbeaten canvas chair Tony had on the roof of his houseboat, his shirt off, working with pencil and paper over the cost factors of his new home. Thalia continued to handle the banking matters, transferring funds to Plover's checkbook as he needed them, so he was not too familiar with the petty details, but he felt he understood the general outlines of their financial situation. He knew that with taxes, insurance, and impounds, they were paying $340 a month for their house, that both cars were paid for, because Plover did not like to owe money, and believed that he was saving money by paying cash.

He estimated another $600 for routine expenses, taxes, etc., and the $500 a month put into stocks, left, out of his monthly salary of $2200, approximately $760 for himself. He felt he could live on $500 a month, and so any error in his calculations would take up the slack. Five hundred dollars. When he had first started out in radio $500 was a dream, an impossible sum. Even now the thought of it made him feel good. Being generous with himself, he decided that he could spend up to $125 on an apartment. But it would have to be a good big one, preferably with a view, because he intended for his children to come and stay with him as often as possible.

Within a few days he discovered nearly all his calculations were wrong. There were no good apartments in Sausalito, or for that matter, in Southern Marin County, for $125. Everyone wanted to live in Marin County, particularly Sausalito, and this drove the prices up out of sight. One-room studios with a gas ring for a kitchen were going for $150, and Plover, at his closest estimate, needed a two-bedroom apartment with a kitchen and a living room. These started at around $300 a month, and Plover was amazed to learn that the people who owned them did not want children on the premises. As he grew more familiar with the want ad section of the paper he began to see that there were five- and six-bedroom houses for rent, no children, no pet. He wondered what anybody would do with all those rooms. (He found out later, and revenge was for once sweet: often the people who held out for adults would rent to a pleasant-looking young couple who would then turn out to be the fronters for a group of hippies or a rock band.)

Very well, he would go to $200, but that was tops. This gave him an excuse to call Thalia, and he made an appointment to visit her and discuss finances. She could hardly refuse. The house was a mess when he got there, shortly after noon. He peeked into the little spare bedroom he had used for a studio, which Thalia now had to herself, and saw the piles of mail, opened and unopened, the stacks of bills, papers, unironed laundry, bolts of material, and balls of yarn, and told Thalia, "I'll wait out on the patio."

"It's a mess," she said. Plover thought she meant the

studio, but she had actually meant the patio. No one had swept the leaves or pulled the grass and weeds from between the loose bricks, and there were various remains from a cookout: a half-cooked and half-sun-melted marshmallow stuck to the bottom step, the big hibachi was still full of ashes, and there were mustard stains on the long low redwood table. Plover was irritated by this mess, but he tried to keep from saying anything, knowing he would only antagonize Thalia if he spoke up. The recent rains had made everything grow, and so the patio area looked a little bit like a jungle setting; when Thalia came out with an armload of papers, he jokingly commented on the shagginess, and before he could shut his mouth he also said, "Boy, this house hasn't been cleaned since I left, has it?"

Thalia sat down and said, "You never did any of the work even when you were here," and started rattling the papers around on her lap. Her lips were pressed tight in anger, and Plover wished he had not come.

"When I did try to help out," he heard himself say, "you always acted as if I was making a worse mess."

"We don't have very much money," she said.

"What do you mean we don't have very much money?"

"Well, we just don't," she said. "We have a lot of expenses."

Plover felt the animal panic reaching into him, and the beginnings of suspicion, a suspicion that would recur every time he began to worry about finances: *Was Thalia salting away his money?* He knew better, of course, but he could not help the thought from coming into his mind, and he could not hold off the panicky feeling.

Thalia began the economics lesson by handing Plover a thick wad of canceled checks, held together by a red rubber band. Most of the checks seemed to be made out to cash, either at the bank or at the Old Town Saloon, in amounts ranging from one hundred dollars to fifteen dollars (which was the maximum the bar would cash). There seemed to be far too many of these. Plover was liberal about buying drinks, but the bar was liberal right back, and he had thought over the years that he had just about broken even with the management. Apparently not. And many of the checks were signed by Thalia rather than himself.

Others were made out to pet clinics, dentists, nurseries, mortgage companies, drugstores, supermarkets (a fantastic amount to the supermarkets), oil companies, garbage companies, newspapers, magazines, telephones, and all the rest of the impedimenta of living. Plover had stopped actually reading the checks and was just sitting thumbing through them while Thalia explained that his check every two weeks amounted to not much over $600, for a monthly total of $1320, out of which he insisted on spending $500 on stocks, leaving Thalia with barely enough to run the household. Her tone was not aggressive or whining or even prim, but simply concerned. She, too, was worried about where the money would come from for them to live apart, and for a long time (it sounded to Plover as if she meant years) she had held back because she did not want to break him. But it was a very real problem, and she did not see how they could solve it.

Until this moment Plover had thought of himself as a rich man, not in the sense of millions, but in the sense that he did not have to worry about money. To him, that was wealth.

Now he made himself see that of his $2200 per month, only the $500 he was putting into stocks was free for him to use. There was no point in selling any of their existing stocks (although that might have to happen when they actually got divorced) but he could not buy anymore. He thought of what his broker might say, and then remembered that his broker had been married two or three times himself.

He said to Thalia, at last, "Well, I guess all I can do is use the stock money."

She nodded as if she had come to the same conclusion some time ago, and was only waiting for him to reach it on his own. This irritated him, so he said, "Unless you'd like to go back to work."

Thalia said very seriously, "I would. But not the same kind of work." Before Plover could brighten to the prospect of Thalia supporting herself, she explained that since she had supported him for several years while he got his college degree, and even worked afterward when he was on commission and not making enough to live, then he should not mind supporting her while she went to graduate school and prepared herself for a career. Plover agreed immediately, not only because it was sensible but because she seemed to think he would not. Of course he would. "Jesus, it's only fair," he said.

16

The next time he looked at the want-ad section of the paper his viewpoint was different and his attitude was humble. As much as he hated to, he even went to look at a few places, from cute cottages that needed a little work (brokendown shacks) to glorious living in sun-drenched Sausalito's most luxurious apartment complex (stucco rooms with a tiny square of view and of course no tots or pets). Plover began to develop a real revolutionary fervor against the kinds of people who owned property for rent.

One place, at two hundred a month, was so ideal in every way except price that he could not pass it up. This was a genuine view apartment, on Bulkley, overlooking the entire bay from San Francisco to Belvedere; three rooms including the kitchen, but the living room was large enough for his children to throw down sleeping bags and be comfortable. The place was light and airy, wood-paneled, and appeared to have been built around fifty years ago. There was parking space outside underneath a huge old oak tree, and altogether the place sang to him and made him want to throw his budget overboard. "I'll take it," he said to the sweet little old lady who owned the place and lived upstairs.

"There will be a four hundred dollar cleaning deposit," she said. She seemed to be looking at Plover's hair, which was a little long. Plover knew all about cleaning deposits; everyone he had talked to about moving had explained that when apartments are at a premium, landlords (that word had new meaning for Plover) would take huge fees and call them cleaning deposits. Plover reddened, thanked the lady, told her he would be in touch, and left. He simply would not allow himself to be hooked through the bag. But that afternoon he looked at two more places, both filthy, dingy and overpriced, and so by six o'clock he put his scruples in his pocket and called the landlady for the Bulkley place. It had been rented not ten minutes after he left. "By a very *nice* young man," she said.

And so it went. There was something wrong with every place he looked at, and after only a week of househunting Plover grew discouraged and depressed enough to call Thalia in the middle of the night and beg her to allow him to come home. It was a miserable telephone conversation, with long embarrassed pauses on both sides, and when Plover finally hung up he wished desperately that he had never called. He was alone on the houseboat and it was well after midnight. He did not want to go downtown to the bar and he did not want to watch television. He knew that he would not be able to get to sleep without smoking some marijuana, but he did not want to do that, either. He admitted to himself that he was a little bit prudish about marijuana. Years before, when he and Thalia had first been married, they used to get stoned nearly every weekend. In those days, the middle fifties, everyone who smoked marijuana was afraid of the police, and paranoia was part of getting high. Just sitting thinking about it, Plover remembered a time when he had been so stoned that when he was taking a leak he passed out straight backward, landing on the bathroom floor with a crash. Thalia rushed in to find him on his back, still holding onto his penis, still pissing, only now straight up into the air, like a fountain.

He laughed, just thinking about it, and went into the kitchen and got Tony's plastic bag of marijuana from its place of concealment behind the toaster. It was not much of a hiding place, but people weren't as paranoid anymore. He sat at the kitchen table, slowly going through the ritual of rolling a joint, trying to remember why he and Thalia gave up smoking dope. Probably it was because of the children. Plover felt that it was not fair to the children to keep dope around the house. What if they got arrested? Who would take care of the children? He licked down the joint and lit it with a kitchen match. The excuse seemed sort of feeble now, but at the time it might have been persuasive enough. But when they went to parties he would not join in if a joint was being passed around, although Thalia would. That wasn't for the children's sake. It was something in himself. There was something prudish in his nature, something that did not like the pleasure marijuana gave. No. That had to be wrong, because he felt nothing about drinking. Well, maybe because it was illegal. Plover sucked deeply on the joint and walked back into the living room, flipping on the television set.

The marijuana was beginning to affect him, and he sat down comfortably and watched Johnny Carson, unable, after the first few minutes, to make much sense out of what he was seeing, but enjoying the company and feeling a rising sense of anticipation and pleasure from the marijuana. It occurred to him, in his dazed and happy state, that he did not actually have to find an apartment in Sausalito, or even in southern Marin, even though the station was in Sausalito. He could live in San Francisco if he pleased, in a nice high-rise view apartment, looking out at the twinkling lights of the city, crossing the Golden Gate Bridge against the commuting traffic, reestablishing himself at Enrico's and his other old city haunts, indeed, making himself a whole new life. He was a city boy, anyway. All this crap about living in the suburbs was a bunch of crap. Horse shit and hay fever, somebody once called it, only he was talking about living in the real country. Actually, Plover had always wanted to live way out in the country, in a big three-story farmhouse surrounded by tall whispering trees, a swimming pool, barn full of horses (although Plover did not ride and his wife and daughters did), and long walks through the woods to a bluff overlooking the sea . . . well, that was out. It didn't make any sense without Thalia. She was the farm girl, not he. Whatever that meant.

On the other hand, and by this time he was not sure how many hands he had used up, he did not have to stay in the Bay Area at all. He could live any goddamn place he wanted. He could always get a job. He was popular. They had talk shows everywhere. He dragged in the sponsors like shit drew flies, and he could do it here, Los Angeles, Chicago, or even New York. He looked at Johnny Carson. They were in the same business. There was no reason, given enough confidence, that Plover could not take Carson's place.

"Wow," he said aloud, "I knew I was stoned, but wow!" He *was* stoned, but he made a note to himself to try to remember in the morning that there was no reason he had to stay in Sausalito, big frog in little pond; he could go to New York and try to be a big frog in the biggest pond. New York!

With that pleasant vision in his head, he drifted out. When Tony got home, alone, at about quarter to three, Plover woke up long enough to greet him pleasantly, undress, and get into his sleeping bag. Tony snickered and asked him if he wanted a hot peanut butter sandwich, and Plover drifted off, thinking, yes, I would like a hot buttered peanut sandwich, but in New York, New Fucking York, not here.

17

Plover and Tony walked into the Old Town Saloon at a little after five o'clock on Sunday afternoon. Tony was dressed for work in dark slacks and white shirt, with a scarf at his throat instead of a necktie, his long curly hair wetted and combed back so that he almost looked civilized. Plover was wearing faded Levis and a red sweatshirt that had washed down to an old-rose color. The bar was half full, and making his way back to the toilet Plover said hello or nodded to at least fifteen people. He felt good; Thalia was not in the place and a lot of his friends were. He and Tony were going to have a drink before going down to the Seven Seas for dinner. Tony went on shift at seven. Plover wanted to talk to Tony about the housing situation, and he felt that dinner would be a good time to do it. Plover fully intended to pay for the dinner.

As a matter of fact Plover ate no dinner that night. Instead he got terribly drunk. It began when the big beefy girl named Mollie came over and without being asked, sat down between Plover and Tony and began talking. Although it had been only a week or so since she had been to bed with Tony, she hardly paid any attention to him, turning instead toward Plover, putting her hand on his wrist and leg to emphasize points and smiling into his eyes. She had strong views on the war in Vietnam, civil rights, and ecology, views Plover had heard until he was sick of them, and, like many of Plover's listeners (obviously she was a listener) she felt that he was not sufficiently aware of the issues or he would take stronger stands. It never did any good for Plover to explain that he did in fact have his own personal views, but on the air he was supposed to be impartial and unprejudiced. At first he was irritated with her, but the way she kept touching him and looking him in the eye had its effect, and Plover for the first time since the breakup began to feel horny. He grinned over at Tony and Tony shrugged and ordered another round of drinks from the barmaid. Plover noticed the barmaid's ass as she walked away from them and felt a surge of pleasure. He was coming alive again, and by God if there was any justice he was going to get laid tonight. Tony would not be home until nearly three, which gave him the houseboat all to himself for hours. Plover looked at his watch. It was not yet six. He smiled at Mollie, who smiled back and squeezed his arm.

After the second round of drinks Tony excused himself,

because he had to eat whether Plover went along or not. Plover laughed and waved Tony off. He was enjoying himself right where he was. The next day, during the hangover's worst period, he wondered why he never seemed to be able to remember that missing dinner nearly always caused trouble. But he was having fun and he felt good and he did not want either to take Mollie to dinner with them or let her get out of his hands. He was dead certain she would go to bed with him. She had gone to bed with Tony, after all. Other friends dropped in and sat with Plover, and by the time Tony got back from the Seven Seas Plover had had four or five beers and was very happy, surrounded by people, laughing and talking, his arm comfortably around Mollie's broad shoulders.

Piecing it all together the next day was doubly difficult. Not only was Plover depressed and anxious from his hangover, he had literally blacked out the night before and could not remember many of the things he had said and done. Tony was some help in filling in the gaps, and so much of what Plover reconstructed was from Tony's point of view.

"You were the life of the party for a while there," Tony told him. "Talking a mile a minute, hugging and kissing old Mollie, bullshitting with the people at all the tables around you. Then along about ten o'clock you lurched to your feet and took off. Where'd you go?"

Plover put his hands over his eyes, but it did not make him feel any better. "I went down to the No Name and called Thalia," he said. He did not tell Tony what he said to her, because all he remembered was an intense feeling of pleasure, of freedom, and the need to go somewhere out of the bar and call her and thank her, to tell her she was right and they were both better off separated. The next time he saw Thalia she told him what he had actually said. "You told me I was a smart bitch, that you were with a girl and that you hoped I was alone and lonely. You said you hoped I would have a lot of lonely nights, and that if I had enough of them it might pay for what I had done to you. You were very vicious."

"Oh, Christ," Plover said. "I didn't mean it."

"I know you didn't," Thalia said.

Then he burst back into the bar, redfaced, mean-looking, still grinning but obviously spoiling for an argument.

Mollie was surrounded by the same people Plover had gathered at his table, but he ignored her and them, going instead down to the other end and standing by the service bar, drinking Dos Equis and talking to the two barmaids. The place was very crowded by now, and there were several others who were just as drunk as Plover. One of them was Terry Simmons, a tight-faced, almond-eyed man of about forty who seldom talked to anybody but sat in a corner of the bar drinking coffee and looking straight ahead. Some weeks before, when he learned who Plover was, he came over and asked to sit with Plover and Thalia, and they had had a fairly lively conversation about American Indians. Because of the Alcatraz invasion, Plover had been getting a lot of calls about Indians, and it turned out that one of his callers was Terry Simmons, who had apparently read every book about Indians ever written.

Simmons seemed to be a very strange man, and Plover usually tried to avoid him. There was an intensity to his eyes and a self-mocking tone to his voice that warned Plover somehow of danger in this man. But outwardly everything was cordial, and after that first evening Plover, whether he wanted to or not, spent time with Simmons. Always the conversation would be about some timely or intellectual subject, and Simmons never bored Plover with commonplace views or abstractions; it seemed, after a while, as if he was challenging Plover to a game of wits —the one who knew the most would win. It became clearer when Plover learned that Simmons had not finished high school, and yet still held down a job as a chemist for Standard Oil over in Richmond. Simmons was as proud of his white-collar status and his book learning as another man might be of holding a world record. And there was an edge to his discussions with Plover; as if he, Simmons, were trying to prove that he would be better at Plover's job than Plover himself. Plover was used to this. "What the hell do you do except talk to people?" he had been asked rhetorically many times. Simmons never put it on this basis, but the challenge was there, nonetheless.

On this night Simmons was drunk, sitting in his usual corner alone, but grinning out at the world, his eyes fixed and glassy. Plover had never seen him even so much as drink before, and he was pleased. Old bastard, he thought, about time he loosened up. Plover asked one of the barmaids to take Simmons a drink, and was surprised and delighted to see that Simmons was drinking Lemon Hart and orange juice. Wow, he thought. When he goes off the wagon he really goes off the wagon. He turned and faced the corner of the bar, holding up his beer bottle and grinning at Simmons, in a silent toast to conviviality.

His own version of what happened next was marred by

97

several blank spots, and Tony's version was hampered by the fact that Tony had been behind the bar. "You turned around and waved your beer bottle at the guy and he must have thought you were threatening him or something because he jumped up with his face all screwed up and tried to get at you. I think he called you a son of a bitch. A couple of guys caught ahold of him and I had you from behind the bar, just my hand on your shoulder. I couldn't see your face, but Sally says you looked as crazy as he did, the two of you, your faces a couple of inches apart, calling each other sons of bitches and bastards and everything else. You took a swing at him but you were a little wide, and somebody caught your arm anyhow. We hustled him out of the bar, and when I turned around you were gone, too. I didn't know where you were until I heard the screaming."

Plover did not remember how he got outside, but he remembered why he had gone and what he did. Somehow, he got the idea that Simmons and Thalia were having an affair. He had remembered the way Simmons had looked at Thalia that one night, the way you should not look at a woman in front of her husband. Plover had been a little irritated at the time, but now, drunk, he decided they were having a full-blown affair and that was why his marriage had broken up. When he saw Simmons coming toward him, passionate with hatred, he knew he was right.

He followed Simmons out into the street, but he could not see him anywhere. Perhaps he was across the street in the parking lot, waiting for Plover behind a parked car. Plover stepped out into the street and yelled, "SIMMONS!" A car came along and Plover moved out to the double yellow line to let it pass. "SIMMONS, YOU MOTHERFUCKER!" Another car came along. Plover gave the driver the finger and walked back to the sidewalk. Obviously Simmons was not going to come out of hiding.

"YOU CHICKENSHIT MOTHERFUCKER, COME OUT AND FIGHT!" Plover leaned up against the building and waited for Simmons to emerge. Perhaps he had not made it strong enough. "SIMMONS, I'M GONNA CUT YOUR NUTS OFF AND STUFF THEM DOWN YOUR FUCKING THROAT!"

Tony came out of the bar and stood next to Plover. "What's the matter?" he asked.

Plover started to cry. "That son of a bitch broke up my marriage," he said. He could feel his face contorting. "God damn it. YOU FUCKING SIMMONS COWARD FUCKER!" he screamed. Tony's hand was on his arm.

"Let me run you back to the houseboat," he said.

"I'll KILL him!" Plover said. "Go back in the fucking bar and leave me alone."

Tony said the next day, "I tried to get you out of there but boy, you wouldn't move. You were sure Simmons was across the street waiting for you with a knife. You kept saying, 'I won't go in the bushes with that fucking bushwacker, but I'll fight him in the street,' and stuff like that, until the two cops showed up."

Plover remembered the two young policemen well enough. They were terribly polite to him, and he remembered seeing them secretly smile at each other, as if they were handling a stubborn child. They did not ask him his name, only what he was doing. "I'm waiting for the guy that broke up my marriage," he said pleasantly. "How are you fellows tonight?"

"We're just fine," one of the policemen said. Neither of them could have been as old as thirty. Plover felt paternal toward them. So many people hated the police, yet here were as nice a pair of kids as you could hope to meet.

The policeman continued, "Don't you think you'd better get off the street? You were making quite a racket there. We got two calls."

"Gee, I'm sorry," Plover said. "Christ, I didn't mean to make any trouble, except for that bastard stole my wife."

Tony said, "The guy he was arguing with went home about ten or fifteen minutes ago. There won't be any more trouble."

"See to it," the policeman said. To Plover he said, "You be nice and quiet now, hear?"

"Wait," Plover said. "I insist on knowing your names and shaking your hands."

Sheepishly, the two officers told Plover their names and let him pump their hands, and then they walked off together, and Plover heard one of them snicker. He went back into the bar with Tony. "No more trouble," he said. "I'm practically sober, anyhow."

He knew he was acting sober, just as he knew the madness had passed, but he was still drunk, and meant to get even drunker yet. He felt delicious, powerful, and happy. Plover looked over the blur of faces and picked out Mollie's at a table near the back. He winked at her and saw her wink back, although a large black man was holding on to her arm and whispering into her ear. Plover made a place for himself at the bar and ordered another beer. Instead, Tony brought him a cup of coffee.

"Wake up and go home," Tony said.

"Am I eighty-six?" Plover asked.

"No."

"Then I want a beer. Come on, for Christ's sake. I'm over it."

Tony left the coffee in place, but brought Plover a beer, which he drank slowly, listening to the conversations around him, feeling warm and alert. After two more beers and no trouble at all, he went to the toilet and on the way back bent down and whispered to Mollie, "Let's go." She excused herself from the table and followed Plover out of the bar.

"Where to?" she said. "Brr, it's cold out here."

"Bracing, refreshing, delightful," he said. He took her shoulder and moved her across the street to the parking lot and into his car. He kissed her on the mouth and felt her breasts while the engine warmed up. "Mmm," she said. "Yummy!"

Plover drove very carefully back to Gate Five. Everything was quiet, except for the muted distant sounds of music from one or two houseboats. The lights sparkled in the night air, and mist hung low over the still water of the bay. The moon was nearly full and glowed within a ring of light. Mollie did not talk, but hung on to Plover's arm warmly. They went down the chickenwalk to Tony's houseboat side-by-side and almost fell off into the water. After Plover helped her aboard he pressed her against the door and kissed her again. "Let's go inside, for heck's sake," she said when they broke the kiss.

Plover remembered very little about the actual love-making, or anything else that happened after they got inside and turned on the heater and the oven. He remembered seeing her emerge naked from a pile of clothing, her skin glowing with pinkness in the candlelight, her arms held out to him, a smile on her lips. Then they were upstairs in Tony's bed making love and then he was lying on his side and she was asleep and snoring slightly, and he was thinking that she was entirely different as a lover than as a person, and he began to respect her and feel warm and affectionate toward her. She had sensed his need for a woman and come to bed with him even though for most of the evening he had ignored her and left her with others. They had said nothing to each other about making love until he pulled her out of the bar, and yet she had known. He drew her toward him, turning her over to face him. She groaned, and he began kissing her neck. He felt her arms come around him, and then she said, "Just a sec, I have to pee-pee," and she got up and padded down the ladder. Plover looked over the edge and saw Tony asleep on the couch. He smiled and felt the beginnings of a headache. It must be late, he thought. But he was going to make love again, twice in one night, a thing he had not done with Thalia in years.

But he did not remember actually having made love again that night. He only remembered getting bored waiting for Mollie to come out of the bathroom and then feeling irritated when she snuggled up to him. By then he was three-quarters asleep again and drifted off without reacting.

He had not set the alarm, but he still woke up at the correct time. He got out of the bed and down the ladder and began to make coffee before he realized that he was still a little drunk and that he had not managed to sleep away any of the impending hangover. He groaned a little in anticipation, dressed himself, and left for the studio without having coffee. As for Mollie, she could take care of herself.

18

The hangover lasted two days. Plover thought he was going to be all right for a while when he got to the studio and had two cups of coffee and a jelly doughnut with Cal Martin the engineer, and Bob Hamilton, Plover's producer. Cal remarked humorously that Plover hadn't seemed to be in any pain the night before, and when Plover looked blank Cal laughed and said, "You probably don't even remember seeing me." Cal had apparently been at the table when Plover came up and grabbed Mollie.

They went on the air and he read his five minutes of news from the edited yellow teletype sheets, played a commercial, and then threw open his telephone. It was just his luck that on this morning all the lines were full.

He felt a light sweat on his forehead, and for a moment he thought he was going to vomit. As a deep-voiced man talked indignantly about student militants Plover wondered if he could make it to the toilet and throw up during a one-minute commercial. He signaled to Cal through the glass, making pitcher-and-glass gestures and Cal grinned and brought him a paper cup full of water. That helped, but not much. The voices—indignant, pleading, self-satisfied, curious, even drunk—buzzed in his ear, and his stomach felt as if he had swallowed a sack of flour. He could taste whiskey, although he hadn't drunk any, and his nose seemed burned out. That came from hanging around places where people smoke tobacco, he thought; as if that mattered. As if anything mattered. He could see himself out in the middle of the main street of Sausalito, screaming filth at Simmons, a man at least three inches taller than himself and ten pounds heavier. A man with homicidal tendencies. Plover touched his cheek, which had the feel of an unripe peach. Standing in the middle of the street, insane drunk, screaming that Simmons had destroyed his marriage. Waves of humiliation and nausea came over him, as the people talked and he listened. When Peggy Lavan came in, wearing a white buckskin sheath minidress, she said, "Boy, you were sure subdued this morning. They walked all over you."

"I guess," he said. He left the booth and went into the bathroom and gratefully threw up. When he came out, after washing himself, he found Fiedler standing in the hall, looking at him sourly. Plover waved at him, grinned in a sickly way and walked past him without speaking. He felt guilty and frightened. Fiedler, once he found out how Plover had been behaving, would probably fire him. And of course Plover deserved firing, after last night. He had the feeling that everyone would hate him, now. He dreaded going back to the houseboat and facing Tony's accusing look and Mollie's smirk. But he had no place else to go.

Plover learned a great lesson that morning: Never smoke marijuana to cure a hangover. He found his symptoms exaggerated, the time lengthened, and his emotional instability increased. Usually marijuana would cut his emotions in half, but now it seemed to have the opposite effect. He could not stop thinking about how he had behaved the night before, and he could not help thinking that the police would be coming to get him soon, that they would throw him in jail, where he deserved to be, and that everyone would feel great contempt for him. Thalia, the one he had always depended on to save him, would no longer do so. He was alone, utterly alone, and he wanted to puke.

Tony was upstairs asleep and Mollie was gone. Plover lay dizzy on the couch wishing a hundred hours would pass. Finally, under the combined influence of half a joint, four aspirins, and a pint of milk, he fell into a light sleep, in which he dreamed over the events of the night before. It was not much of an improvement, but he knew he was asleep and dreaming, and that helped. From previous experience he believed the hangover would end soon and he would feel euphoric all afternoon and then sentimental that night. His hangovers had always been the same. On the nights after hangovers he would sit and watch television, weeping at everything. His theory was that his emotional strength had been used up by the alcohol and the hangover, and that sentimentality is what you felt when your emotional strength was gone.

This time it was different. When he awakened he was still hung over. He still felt guilty and harassed, and he wondered if perhaps he was an alcoholic. He had several of the symptoms he had read about: blacking out, terrible hangovers, change of personality. That would mean he could no longer drink, or it would just get worse and worse. But he could not face the thought of not drinking. His whole social life seemed to revolve around drinking. It was awful. With a sickening feeling in his stomach he realized that he could not go back to the Old Town Saloon anyway, after the incredible ass he had made of himself. So he might as well quit drinking. He had to give everything else up. No more friends, no more wife, no more children, his boss about to fire him. He could even envision the speech in which Fiedler did it:

"Plover, you hardly do a day's work around here as it is. You waltz in the door, open the lines, and waltz out again in three hours. For this you receive a fantastic wage. It's enough money, I think, for us to be able to ask of you a certain standard of conduct, both in the station and outside. After all, you are something of a public figure, although I can't understand why. So when it's called to my attention (here pointing to a stack of letters and telegrams on the desk) that you've been standing in the middle of Bridgeway screaming profanity, I begin to wonder whether we can't dispense with your services after all. . . ."

Nor could Plover avoid the image of himself down on his knees in front of Fiedler, begging for his job back.

He looked out at the blue bay reflecting sky, and he

happened to notice the rowboat. It had been there all the time, but it had never occurred to Plover that it was actually a boat that you could go rowing in. He wondered if it was safe to go rowing on the bay, although he often saw people out rowing, even girls. With a sneer at himself for cowardice, he opened the glass doors and stepped down into the rowboat. It rocked slightly, but from the feel of it under his feet, Plover knew it would not tip over easily. He sat down and put the oars into the oarlocks, untied the line, and, with the tip of one oar, clumsily pushed off. He had not been rowing in twenty years.

For the next hour Plover rowed and drifted among the channels of Gate Five, seeing the houseboat community from an entirely different perspective. From the shore and from the boardwalks, Gate Five appeared as a filthy collection of shacks and half-sunken hulks, a ghetto over the water, an unsafe area filled with shabby and dirty people. From the water everything seemed more natural, and Plover began to notice the potted plants that seemed to grow everywhere. Nearly every houseboat had pots full of succulents, or even tubs of them, their thick green leaves fatly proliferating, their yellow or red flowers tiny but bright against the worn paint of the boats. It struck Plover that Gate Five was very colorful and did not smell nearly as bad as he had always thought. Perhaps he was just getting used to it.

With the sun hot on his back, and the steady pull of the oars against his unexercised muscles, Plover felt better than he had all day, in fact, the hangover seemed to have ended. He even felt useful, as if rowing was a task of more real value than his job. And he was not alone. Once, two girls in bright but ragged clothing went by in a little rowboat, sitting side-by-side. They waved and smiled at him, and he waved and smiled back, noting that he was a better rower than they were. Another time, a man wearing a black cape, with long greasy hair and a long graying beard, with a face like a combination of Moses and Fagin, rowed by with an orange tomcat resting calmly on the back seat of his boat. Plover smiled at the man and the man said, "Hodda fuck ahyah!" Plover noticed that the man's thin bare arms were knotted with hard muscle. He wanted to call out, "What do you do for a living?" but had the sense not to.

After a while his own arms, which were not knotted with muscle, began to feel sore, and his headache returned, even worse than before. He rowed slowly back to Tony's boat. Tony was awake and helped him dock the boat. In spite of his headache, Plover was eager to describe his row, including a description of the man who had said, "Hodda fuck ahyah!"

"Oh, that's Captain Poontang," Tony said. "He's sort of the mayor of Gate Five."

"Captain Poontang?" Plover was offended by the name.

Tony said, "You look kind of pale." Plover had expected Tony to be angry with him, but he did not seem to be. He wore the usual smug look of amusement and tolerance of someone who does not have a hangover in the presence of someone who does. Hangovers were very comical if you did not happen to have one.

Later that afternoon Plover managed to get to sleep. He dreamed about Captain Poontang. The man was grinning like a Jewish satyr and in his thick Brooklyn accent was inviting Plover to join him. Plover did not know what he was being asked to join; he only knew he was frightened. The man kept saying, "Dere's nuttin to be afraid of," and making that same jerking gesture with a claw-like hand. Plover awakened with relief, and then the relief faded as he felt the headache and stomach ache returning, along with the deep chest pangs of anxiety and guilt. The hangover was still in full force although it was dark out. Plover felt a moment of despair; if he went back to sleep he knew it would be to dream of Captain Poontang's mysterious invitation, and if he stayed awake he would be in agony. He could not drink nor could he smoke marijuana. There was no one to talk to. No one liked him anyway.

Plover made himself a bowl of canned minestrone and sat eating by himself, thinking about New York again. He knew a man who worked in the ABC news department. Plover had something of a reputation; he had been written up in *Advertising Age*. He wouldn't have any trouble getting work in New York. It was positively pleasant to daydream about New York. Plover turned on the television, and after a while he got out the marijuana and smoked himself into a fog. In the morning he awakened full of guilt and self-hatred, the hangover still working in him, and went to work and listened to his callers excoriate each other, barely troubling to interfere. He let one caller rant for ten minutes before the engineer's signal got through to him. Then he buttoned the caller off and was into another call before he realized that he was supposed to be leading into a commercial. He smiled at Cal Martin and buttoned the new caller out with a blunt, "Sure, thanks."

After work he tried to slink out of the place without

talking to anybody, but Fiedler caught him in the hall and asked him to step into his office.

Fiedler sat down and immediately began to twirl the bears around the cobra. Plover watched the bears as they bounced and swung around.

"Listen," Fiedler said, "Are you okay?"

"Sure. What do you mean?"

"Well, Christ, you're going through a hell of a lot. Tougher guys than you have cracked up, you know."

Plover looked right at Fiedler. There seemed to be some real concern in Fiedler's eyes, even though his mouth was still fixed in its bitter twist. My God, is he feeling *sorry* for me? Plover thought. Of course! At once he felt better. "Just fine," he said. "You know. A little pain when I laugh it up too much."

Fiedler said, "Sure, sure. But I think maybe it would be a good idea if you took a little bit of a vacation. You're really shitty on the air these days."

And so it was decided that Plover would take a month's vacation (his regular vacation, but two months early) with full pay. Fiedler recommended that he go to the beach or the mountains, pick up chicks, get drunk, and enjoy life for a while. "You're too damned serious, kid," he said. Plover, of course, knew that he was going to New York to look for another job, thus stabbing Fiedler in the back for being kind to him. He called Thalia that afternoon and told her he was going to New York. "Confidentially, I'm thinking of moving back there," he said.

"Maybe that would be a good idea," she said.

He told Tony, also, in the strictest confidence. "Christ, I can't find any place to live around here," he cracked.

"I envy you," Tony said. "I haven't got the guts."

"I thought you'd been to New York," Plover said.

"I have. I haven't got the guts to go *back*," he said.

Plover was having second thoughts, and daydreaming about a month in Acapulco, when, two mornings later, he opened his morning *Chronicle* to read in Herb Caen's column: "Sausalito talk man Franklin Plover heads for New York soon to consult with ABC brass." Which meant he had to go. He did not, after all, want to make a liar out of Herb Caen.

19

Plover's friend at ABC New York was named Jack Raiford. He and Plover had known each other since college days at San Francisco State, and although they had been good friends neither had written or called since Raiford left KRON-TV in San Francisco to work for the ABC-TV news department. When Plover finally reached him in New York, Raiford was delighted to hear from him and insisted that when Plover arrived he must stay at Raiford's apartment on West 20th. Plover did not say he and Thalia had broken up or that he was coming to New York to find a job. Raiford said, "It's about goddamn time you took a vacation," and Plover let him think so.

It was impossible for him to get out of Marin county

without saying good-bye in person to his children, and so as long as he had to go over to the house anyway he took along his dirty laundry and most of his other clothes and asked Thalia to pack for him. He had not packed anything for himself in a dozen or more years, he explained. She was cheerful about doing it, however, and while he sat out on the patio with the children, she ironed his dress shirts. In the laundry room a month's dirty underwear was in the machine. Instead of washing his own clothes, or taking his laundry downtown, as Tony did, Plover simply bought new underwear and threw the dirty into his blue laundry bag. There was something about doing his own laundry that seemed terribly final to Plover, and he was not the only one. A photographer who hung around the Old Town Saloon told him one day that his ex-wife had done his laundry until he remarried, a matter of three and a half years. Plover hoped it would not be that long with him, even if he and Thalia never did get back together.

There was so much dirty laundry and ironing to do that Plover had to come back the next day—the day he was due to fly out—and pick up his packed bag. When it was all done and his bag was in the back of the car, he realized that he would be gone a month and his car would be sitting in the garage at the airport. "Listen," he said to Thalia, "would you drive me to the airport?" He explained to her what the problem was, and with a slight frown she agreed to take him. It was an hour drive, and for most of the way they did not talk. Plover was suffering from his usual trip anxiety, and on top of it, he was beginning to worry about whether Thalia would kiss him good-bye. In the past when he had taken trips he had not wanted to be kissed good-bye, especially in front of people, but today he did not think he could stand it if she did not move toward him lifting her mouth to be kissed as he opened the car door to get out.

They were driving through San Bruno when Thalia said, "I think it's a very good idea for you to be gone for a month. It will give both of us a chance to breathe and to think." They talked cheerfully, then, for the rest of the drive, about their mutual need for this separation, and how it would take the pressure off both of them, and when they swung up the drive to the outgoing passenger ramp Plover pulled the car up into a yellow zone and jerked on the hand brake and smiled at Thalia and leaned over to kiss her. She turned so that he kissed her cheek. He started to say something but stopped. She was not looking at him. He got his suitcase out of the back and left the car without saying good-bye at all.

Plover was depressed and anxious most of the way across the country, brooding about his marriage and worrying, as he always did, about whether they would crash. The in-flight movie, which he had been counting on to distract him, turned out to be a domestic comedy, and he could not bear to watch it. He switched the ear plugs to classical music and closed his eyes to the film, but he was not able to sleep. He wondered if perhaps he shouldn't have gotten high on marijuana before he left. He had thought about it, but rejected the idea on the grounds that it might accentuate his fear rather than make him feel good.

Seeing New York City from the air, at night, the glittering towers appearing and disappearing among thin clouds, helped to bring him out of his depression. This was, after all, the true capital of the world, and instead of feeling like a middle-aged man fleeing his troubles, he began to feel once more like a young man on his way to conquer destiny. It was good to feel that way again, even falsely, and when he met Jack Raiford in front of the American terminal he was pleased but not surprised when Raiford laughed and said, "Hey, Jesus, you look great!" Plover admitted to himself that he *felt* great.

Because of the feeling, and because Raiford talked all the way home in the cab about what he had been doing and what a terrific place New York was, Plover put off telling him about the splitup, and let Raiford continue thinking he was on vacation. Tomorrow would be soon enough to talk about serious matters.

But tomorrow was spent in hangover. After Raiford had taken Plover to his apartment on West 20th and dropped his suitcase, he insisted on taking him down to the Village, to Casey's, where they drank and chatted with Raiford's friends until three in the morning. Both of them were drunk when they got back to the apartment, but Raiford insisted that they have a nightcap, and got out his bottle of bourbon. "We'll talk till dawn," he said. "Just like the old days." They did not quite make it till dawn, but when Plover awakened it was only nine o'clock. He was still dressed, lying on the couch under a quilt. He got up and made his way to the bathroom to get a drink of water. Raiford was sitting in the bathtub in gray sudsy water, looking grim. Raiford had been a tall handsome muscular man when Plover had known him before, but now he seemed to have gotten pale and pudgy through the middle, just like Plover himself. He looked up and said good morning. Plover drew a drink of water from the tap. It was the worst-tasting water he could remember having drunk. Raiford said, "I got to be to work by ten. Jesus God."

"I don't." Plover said. "Can I use the bed?"

"Sure. In fact, you can use it all week. I have to go to Washington for a few days on assignment. You'll have the joint to yourself."

It did not seem like the proper time to bring up either separation or work, so Plover let it go.

20

Raiford's apartment was in the Chelsea district, on West 20th between Eighth and Ninth, a block of four- and five-story buildings. The street was narrow and gloomy most of the day and filled with people. Plover looked down on them from Raiford's fourth-floor window, and listened to the sounds of the radios, arguments, automobiles, and laughter that drifted up, along with the muggy smells of New York. On one of the front stoops across the street, Raiford had told him, a man had been murdered the day before Plover arrived. Sitting in Casey's, with the white tablecloths and the silver chandeliers the story had sounded tough and entertaining, and remote; but now, looking down on the street and seeing the people (friends and relatives?) drinking beer, sitting on stoops or leaning against cars, the story seemed terrible and ugly.

A black man of about fifty, wearing a white shirt open at the throat, had come out onto the stoop of his building at around twilight. He seemed to be drunk. He was singing a song, and no one paid any attention to him until he began to piss down the front steps. Even then, people reacted only by moving slowly away. The man waved his penis so that the stream of piss rose and fell, and the man laughed. Down the street came another man, a Puerto Rican. His head was bent forward and he was walking rapidly, dressed in a dark suit. He was struck by some of the urine. He jumped sideways cursing with surprise, and when he looked up and saw the laughing black man and knew he had been pissed on, he shouted a curse and started up the steps. Halfway up the steps he stopped and waved his fist and shouted, "God damn, you can't go pissing on people like that!" Perhaps halfway up the steps he saw that the black man was drunk and hadn't pissed on him on purpose; so he stopped, but he was still angry enough to curse at the man, still so full of emotion that he had to do something, if only shake his fist.

The black man tucked away his penis and slowly zipped up his pants while the Puerto Rican stood halfway up the steps. Then the black man smiled broadly and said, "You are not man enough to stop me." He seemed to pause here, and then added, louder, "You goddamn Puerto Rican."

Then the Puerto Rican did what seemed to be a very strange thing; he took off his coat, and holding it like a matador's cape, said to the black man, *"Ha ha, toro!"*

119

Probably he took off the coat to shake the piss off it, and got the idea to insult the black man by playing matador. The black man looked around, as if at an audience, and then smiled. "Ha toro *shit!*" he said. He put his hand into his pocket. The Puerto Rican stepped backward and slowly down the stairs until he was on the sidewalk. "You come on down here, toro," he said contemptuously. "You come on down here and see what happens to you." He stood in his white shirt, his dark coat in his hands, giving little jerks to the coat and saying, *"Ha ha, toro!"* The black man stood at the top of the steps, one shoulder lifted, the other dropped, his hand still in his pocket. He seemed to want to go back into the building. After all, he had only stepped outside to piss. Now he could not go back inside because there was a sarcastic man at the foot of the steps waving a coat at him. He took out his knife and opened it up. "You better get away from here," he said to the Puerto Rican.

This seemed to make the Puerto Rican terribly mad. Without dropping his coat he yelled, *"Why goddamn you, I don't have to do anything you say! You goddam come out and piss on people and give them orders! Fuck you, you black bastard!"*

"You better not call me that," the black man said. He came down the steps waving the knife loosely. The Puerto Rican backed away as the black man descended, but then when the black man was two steps from the bottom, the Puerto Rican suddenly threw his coat to the sidewalk and stepped forward and took the knife away from the drunken black man and stabbed him in the chest, once. The black man yelled, "Oh!" and fell to the sidewalk on his face. His legs drew up like a frog's and then straightened and he did not move anymore. The

Puerto Rican picked up his coat and walked about ten steps in the direction he had been going in the first place, and then slowed down and turned and came back, looking upward at nothing, and sat down on the steps beside the dead man and waited for the police.

At Casey's it had been an anecdote, something to frighten the tourist with, and the other New Yorkers at the table had immediately countered with New York savagery stories of their own. But now looking down on the street Plover really felt it, and he was frightened indeed, not at New York, but at man. And yes, at New York. He was going to have to go out onto that street. Either that, or hole up in the apartment until Jack Raiford came back. He turned away from the window. The apartment was not very cheerful. It had plaster walls, some painted white and some light green. There were a few reproductions and a few posters tacked to the walls. The living room had a low Danish-style couch and coffee table, one orange butterfly chair and one low Danish-style easy chair without arms. A few paperback books lined up on the floor under the window, and papers and magazines scattered around completed the decor. Except for the three locks on the front door. Even so, Raiford had said the night before that he had been knocked over once. The burglar got his television set and some worthless cuff links. "Junkies," Raiford had said. "They'll steal anything."

Plover spent the day frightened, hung over, and exhausted. He wished he had not come to New York. He did not want to live here. He could not stand the idea of living here. There would be no work for him. Sausalito was where he belonged. He had a place in Sausalito. He was known and respected. Let Thalia be the one to move away. But no. The children had a right to continue school right where they were. Plover was the one to move. But not here. Not New York. What a filthy ugly place. What a sick place.

On impulse he telephoned Thalia, to let her know he had arrived all right. In the back of his mind he knew he had held off telephoning her so that she might worry about him, and, worrying, realize that she still cared for him. But she was cheerful enough on the telephone, did not seem worried or even particularly glad to hear from him. She turned him over to the children after only a few sentences, and so after he had spoken to both girls he asked to speak to Thalia again. He wanted to tell her how he felt, all this distance from her, and tell her that he still loved her. He wanted her to know that. But when she got back on the phone all he said was, "Some guy got killed here, across the street, just before I got here. The guy was murdered."

Thalia said, "I was just about to go to the store. Be sure to say hello to Jack for me."

Plover hung up with his face reddening and heating up. He wished Thalia were in the room so he could punch her in the face. Of course he had never hit her or anything like it, but now he wanted to. She did not even care. She was throwing it all away, and for nothing.

He got dressed, knowing he was going to go outside and feeling the anxiety rising in his chest. He made sure he had the key, unlocked the inside locks, and went out. By keeping his eyes straight ahead he made it as far as the corner of Ninth and 20th, but on the corner a man separated himself from a group and came over to Plover.

"You want to buy a couple packs of cigarettes for half a buck?" the man said. He held up two packs of Pall Malls.

"No, thank you," Plover said. "I don't smoke."

The man walked back to his group. "He don't smoke," he said. Plover crossed the street and walked up to a little shop that sold newspapers. He bought the *Times*, the *Post*, and the *Daily News*. He did not like the looks of any of the people he saw on the street. The group of men containing the cigarette seller looked like winos. Plover crossed the street so that he did not have to pass them again, but this brought him past five or six teen-age Puerto Ricans. Plover felt tense as he walked past them, but nothing happened. The boys were talking Spanish and laughing, and paid no attention to him. When he got back up to the apartment he daringly left two of the three locks unlocked. He felt almost like a New Yorker.

21

Plover walked into Casey's a little before midnight. The place was busy but not crowded. He sat at the bar and drank a bottle of Falstaff. He had spent most of the earlier part of the evening searching Jack Raiford's apartment, hoping to find some marijuana. He found nothing. Apparently Raiford's life was an open book. There was nothing in the apartment at all that needed to be hidden. Unless Raiford had a hiding place Plover could not find. But Plover doubted it. It was not that kind of apartment.

Without television (the set had been stolen) and without dope, Plover was at a loss as to how to spend the evening, since he did not want to go outside after dark. But finally he could stand it no longer and so he bathed, dressed, and walked to the corner of Ninth to catch a cab. He had the usual visitor's bad luck with the cab. The first one he flagged down was taken by a woman who appeared from nowhere and got into the cab as Plover held the door open. It was like something out of a bad movie, but it happened. The next two cabs were stopped and taken by men who stepped out between parked cars halfway up the block. Plover was about to try it when a cab pulled up and stopped right in front of him, its light out. The passenger was a black man dressed in a dark suit with a pale gray hat. He paid off the driver, also black, and stepped out as Plover held the door for him. Plover said, "Lucky break for me," and the passenger leaned toward him and whispered, "He's drunk." Plover got in anyway.

The driver might have been drunk or not, but he took Plover directly to 10th Street and let him off in front of Casey's without saying anything at all. Plover reflected, as he drank his beer, that the black passenger might have been the first New Yorker to say anything nice to him. Or he might have been pulling Plover's leg. It did not matter. Plover had already decided that he was going to spend tomorrow deciding where he would go from here, since he obviously did not want to stay in New York. The idea of actually working here was a joke. He wondered where on earth he could go. He did not want to leave the country. It was expensive, and besides, he would have to get a passport, take a bunch of shots, and he did not know what else. It was not worth it. He had not lost anything in Europe. But of course he could not go back to San Francisco or Sausalito now, after only a few days. Everyone would think he had come East looking for a job and had not been able to find one. In fact, everyone was going to think that anyway, no matter when he came home. Then it occurred to him that he did not have a home to go back to. He lifted his empty glass to the bartender, grinning crookedly, like Errol Flynn, and the bartender brought him another beer.

But he was in no mood for self-pity. The other people in Casey's were interesting to watch and included a few minor celebrities, off-Broadway playwrights, magazine writers, actresses and actors, and some of the people who are well known only because they are well known, as Jack Raiford had explained the night Plover arrived. Plover considered himself a bit of a minor celebrity, and so he did not feel like either a tourist or an outsider. Of course he was not known. Pretty well known out on the Coast, though. Well, maybe not on the Coast. That usually meant Hollywood. Better known around San Francisco. *Extremely* well known in Sausalito, a little-known community just the other side of the Golden Gate Bridge. Cute town. Sort of a junior Provincetown. *My* burg, if anybody's asking.

"Aren't you Frank Plover?" a girl said to him. He turned around on his bar stool to see a blond in her middle twenties smiling at him.

"Yes," he said. "Do I know you?"

She laughed. "You were pretty drunk. I met you at the Old Town Saloon in Sausalito about a year ago. I was with Manfred Harris."

Plover did not know who Manfred Harris was, but he nodded and smiled, and when she invited him to join her table he said he would be honored, and followed her to the back room.

"I saw you sitting up there daydreaming when I went to the john," she said.

"Aha," Plover said for no reason at all. She introduced him to some men and women, none of whose names he remembered, and then when he sat down next to her she laughed and said, "Honestly, this is the funniest man in the world. Or at least he was the night I met him."

Plover tried to look like the funniest man in the world on an off or unfunny night. He wished the girl had mentioned her own name. Obviously she was impressed by Plover, and she was good-looking enough for anybody.

"My God, you should have heard him," she began. As she told her story, Plover remembered fragments of the evening she had been talking about. One of those blackout drunk nights, when he had stopped in at the Old Town for a simple before-dinner cocktail and then skipped dinner and drank until closing time. Sometimes Plover could do this and it would be all right; other times, when he was under some kind of stress or anxiety, he would get blind staggering drunk and say or do things he regretted bitterly the next day. As the girl told her story, laughing and exaggerating, Plover remembered more and more of the details, his face flushing at the remembrance. He looked at the other people in the group. They seemed to be enjoying the story without thinking Plover was a fool. They *seemed* to be. Plover could not be sure, since he was convinced that the story made him out to be a perfect asshole.

They had all been sitting back against the wall at two joined tables, and someone had turned the conversation to three-way sex. Plover had told the story of a friend of his, Danny Davis, embellishing it only slightly. Danny Davis and his wife had broken up three or four years ago and were living in different cites, Danny in Sausalito and his wife in San Francisco, and so they saw very little of each other. One night they happened to be invited to the same party, at a large hilltop home in Mill Valley. Danny had come stag and his wife's escort did not want to leave early, and so they found themselves driving down the mountain together, alone with one another for the first time in months. There had been a lot of liquor and marijuana at the party, and both of them felt very good, and they had been talking nostalgically about the past, and so it seemed natural to pull over in a grove of redwoods and make love in the back seat of the car, like teen-agers. It was very exciting for both of them. They had never done this or anything like it when they had been married. After it was over they drove down to the No Name bar in Sausalito and sat out on the patio and talked. They no longer loved each other. But they could have sex, and it could be very exciting. That was one of the things that had been wrong with their marriage; the sex hadn't been exciting. This was only partly because she was frigid. He had not seemed to have made enough of an effort to get her out of it. But that had been the past. Now was the present, and she admitted that she had almost had an orgasm. She had had a couple of orgasms since leaving him, and she felt that she was opening up sexually. He, too, was excited by what had happened between them. There had been something spontaneous and thrilling about it; yet he had always remembered making love in cars or in the woods as being furtive and uncomfortable. Perhaps he, too, was opening up.

He did not remember, or did not tell Plover, which of them brought up the idea of three-way sex, but once the idea had come up it seemed to excite them both. If only they had been able to even think of such a thing when they had been married. They both knew it was too late for the marriage, but it was not too late for them as lovers.

"Do you really mean it?" Danny said.

She nodded her head. "I've really changed a lot," she said.

"Well, listen, I think I know a girl who'd maybe be interested in going to bed with us."

Danny's wife frowned slightly. "A girl?" she said.

"Well, what did you think? Another *guy?*"

"Uh, yes."

Danny bit his knuckle and leaned forward so that no one could hear him. "No, listen, you got it all wrong. Three-way is two chicks and a guy. The other way's *stupid.*"

"I don't see why," she said stubbornly. "What's the difference?"

"Two guys and a girl is *queer,* that's what!" Danny said loudly. People looked at him and he forced himself to grin.

"It isn't any queerer than two girls and a man," she said. She could not be convinced by anything Danny said. He told her that American society had glorified the female body, the female essence, in thousands of millions of photographs, poems, advertisements, movies, television, everywhere, so that it wasn't at all unnatural for girls to be as influenced by it as men. "From the time we're old enough to look at pictures we're brainwashed practically into believing in the innate beauty of the female body. But not *men*," he said.

"You just see it that way because you're a man," she said. And they did not go to bed together again, either as a couple or a triple.

Plover thought it was an outrageously funny story, and obviously that was why he had told it; and why the girl here in Casey's was telling it now; but he also thought it was kind of vicious to tell on his friend Danny, who had taken him into his confidence. Of course he did not mention Danny or his wife by name, but the effect was the same; somebody who heard it could have guessed who it was if he had known either of them. It was *copping out*. But nobody who heard it seemed to think so. The next morning Plover suffered his usual guilty hangover, momentarily expecting Danny to telephone him and say he was coming over to beat hell out of him.

After the story had been told, and everyone at the table had laughed, the girl went on: "After that, he really got funny." She turned to Plover. "Didn't you? Tell them what you were saying."

"I honestly don't remember," Plover said. "I was really drunk."

She did not take the hint. "God, he was funny. He kept saying he'd take any two girls out of the place and show them how it was done, and he kept grabbing at the cocktail waitresses and the other girls walking past and yelling at them, what were you yelling?"

"I don't remember," Plover said desperately.

"Oh, I remember. 'Any you girls wanna sangwich?' Wasn't that it?"

"Something like that, I guess," he said.

"Oh, you were funny as hell," she said.

It was Plover's first experience with what he later called "The New York Knife Job." He could see that the girl had started out to be nice to him, to invite him, the obvious stranger, over to her table, and then to tell a story about him that would make him less a stranger, and then she went on with the story even when she knew it made him appear gross and stupid. There was no reason for it, but he could tell from the way others at the table looked, that he was being knifed and that he would be judged by these people on what he did in return. He wanted their approval and so he grinned at the girl, who had just finished her remarks, and said, "I remember now. You were the only one willing to go along with me."

He said this with apparently the proper tone, because everybody but the girl laughed, and then she laughed too. But he could tell he had done her in. He wondered, really, how. Such a remark would have been taken humorously in California.

"I was just kidding," he said, and he reached out and touched the girl on the wrist. She winked at him.

"Too bad," she said.

The heat was taken off Plover when a party of semi-celebrities entered the room and sat at a table nearby. Everyone watched them until the waiter left with their order, and then one of the men at Plover's table told an anecdote about one of the celebrities, and the conversation drifted into general New York gossip, and Plover was left comfortably alone. He was not left out of things, though. One of the girls, whose name he did not remember, kept looking at him on punch lines and laugh lines, sharing her laughter with him. He always made a point of looking over at her, too, and after an hour had passed, he was certain she wanted him to take her home. The only trouble was, he did not know who she was with. The man on her left was short and fat, wore his hair too long, and had a yellow vest with stains on it. It couldn't be him. He was apparently some kind of magazine editor or writer. The man on her right was thin, his face the color of typing paper, dressed in corduroy. His hair, like Plover's, was receding, but to cover this he combed it forward in a sweep, so that it curled down almost to his eyebrows. It was a useless deception, because his hair was so thin you could see the scalp beneath, white and cold-looking. Plover caught neither his name nor his occupation, but he assumed that he was *the girl's* escort. The blond girl was obviously with the man sitting on her other side, who for some reason Plover thought looked like a tire salesman.

The girl was not precisely a girl. She was at least thirty-five, and probably a bit older. She had dark hair shot with silver, a thin delicate neck and large striking gray eyes that looked almost black in the subdued light of the restaurant. She had good teeth and a delightful laugh, and Plover was very excited by the looking game they were playing with each other, and did not stop to think, until he had gone downstairs to the men's room, that she, too, might be playing some cheap kind of New York trick on him, sharing the laughs and promising much, hoping he would fall for the bit and she could humiliate him. He pissed angrily and went back upstairs, a little drunk but crafty, and ready to take these New Yorkers on their home ground.

22

Her name was Nicole, but her friends called her Kolya, and she had been married four times. Plover never understood why she had taken a liking to him, but it did not matter because she had. When he got back from the toilet she had continued sharing her enjoyment with him, and finally she leaned over and whispered something to the man Plover had assumed was her escort, and then when he nodded and smiled wearily, she gathered her purse and cigarettes and stood up, saying that she had to go. The last person she looked at and spoke to was Plover.

"I'm very glad to have met you," she said, and held her hand out so that Plover would have to half stand to take it. She kept looking into his eyes, and he found himself saying, "May I help you to your car?"

They moved through the crowded bar, Plover close enough behind her to smell her hair. By the time they got to the front door he had three-quarters of an erection. Outside, she turned around and smiled up at him. "I don't happen to have a car. If you'd like, you could walk me home. I only live a few blocks from here."

"I'd be delighted," Plover said. He wished he could remember her name.

She had an apartment on Hudson Street, on the west side of the Village, up only one flight of stairs and overlooking a small garden court. Everything in the apartment seemed to have come from earlier centuries, dull metal, faded glass, worn wood, dimly patterned rugs; even the shelved books and record jackets seemed somehow to come from an earlier time. It was a beautiful room, the kind of room Plover had always wanted to have, but never had. He wondered if it was because of himself or Thalia. Or perhaps the children. Young children would destroy a room like this. "Do you have any children?" he asked, raising his voice. His hostess was in the kitchen opening a couple of bottles of beer.

"Lord yes," she said. "Seven of them."

Plover looked around the darkened living room, as if expecting the children to come out of the shadows. "Where are they?" he asked.

She entered with the beers and handed him one. "In school, various places," she said. The seven children, she told him as they sat on the couch looking down at the garden, were divided between three fathers, and all were in boarding schools.

"I live for my summers," she told him. "I have a house in Cape Cod and we all get together for the whole summer. In fact, I'll be leaving for there in just a few weeks."

Plover had gotten over his surprise about the seven children, and he was no longer interested in talking about them. What he needed was to know her name, so that when he took her hand and moved over close to her, he could breathe it into her ear. He did not feel right about trying anything if he did not know her name. But she continued to talk about her house in Cape Cod and how much she looked forward to being with her family, until Plover finished his beer. He did not want to ask her for another one directly, so he bent the can, as a hint, and set it on the side table.

"Don't you smoke?" she asked him.

He told her all about quitting smoking, and then, before he could stop himself, he told her all about Thalia and their broken marriage. He unburdened himself fully, and by the time he was finished it was dawn and he had drunk two more beers and he knew her name. And she knew everything there was to know about him, because he had spilled his guts all over her. He had done the one thing you do not do with a woman—talk about the previous woman—and when it was all over and she told him he would have to go, he said, "Listen, I'm sorry about the confessional hour."

"I understand," she said. "I'm the first woman you've talked to."

"Yes."

"Kiss me."

They kissed and held each other tightly for a moment.

"Now you have to go," she said.

135

They kissed again and Plover said, "I want to see you again."

"Call me," she said. "But right now I have to walk my dog."

While Plover waited, she brought the dog, a small black and red dachshund, out of the back of the apartment on a leash. She carried the dog down the steps, and Plover opened the front door to the building. It was light out, but there weren't any people on the street. Kolya put the dog on the sidewalk and her hand under Plover's arm and they walked slowly to the corner.

"You can wait for a cab, but I don't know if you'll have much luck at this hour," she said. "Where do you live?" He told her and she said, "Oh, that's not too far," and showed him which way to walk. He kissed her again and left her at the corner. He walked rapidly. It seemed wonderful to be walking up Ninth Avenue in the dawn light.

He called her at eleven in the morning, and she seemed glad to hear from him. He invited her to dinner, saying, "I don't know the town, so you'll have to be the escort," and she said she would be glad to be of service. Plover spent the rest of the day idly, as a tourist, wandering around the midtown section, gaping at the buildings and the people, happy to be footloose and alone. When he went back to the apartment to shower and change, he did not even feel any qualms about walking down the street.

They had a couple of martinis at her apartment before going out, and Plover kissed her while they were standing in the kitchen and she laughed and hugged him and got

away. He kissed her again in the taxi and while she returned the kiss she did not seem interested in continuing.
She leaned forward in the seat, her hand on the back of
the front seat, and instructed the driver on every turn, as
they moved uptown and east. Plover thought this was just
a slightly unpleasant aspect of her character until he
learned that most New Yorkers do the same thing in self-
defense. They had dinner in a small, dark, and pleasant
Italian restaurant in the East Fifties, and then, at Plover's suggestion, they went down to Casey's again. It was
not crowded, and they were shown to a small table near
the front. Plover would have liked to have held her hand,
but he did not.

On the night before, he had told her all about his dis-
solving marriage; tonight, he told her all about his career, and she asked him if he was in New York looking
for a job. He decided he was, and told her he hoped to
get out of radio and into television, and as he said it he
began to believe it, and she told him all about the people
she knew in the television and movie businesses. By one
o'clock Plover was half drunk and wanted to get her out
of there. "Are you ready to go home?" he asked her. She
nodded yes, rather shyly, and he escorted his precious
companion out into the sharply cold night.

At her place it took them a few minutes just to warm
up. Apparently, New York's spring weather was
changeable. Finally, Kolya said, "Would you like to take
off your coat?"

Plover said, "Let's walk the dog, as long as we're
dressed." He did not mean for it to come out quite that
way, but she did not seem to notice. She got the dog from
wherever she kept him (a made-over pantry, he learned

later) and they took him out onto the windy chilly street. Plover saw two other people walking dogs. When they got back to the apartment and took off their coats, Plover played with the dog while Kolya made hot brandies. The dog's name was Reddy. He had been named by Kolya's son Charles, who was either her eldest son or her eldest son by her second marriage, Plover was not sure which. He could not get her family affairs straight, and so far had not tried to.

They drank their drinks, side-by-side on the couch, looking out at the treetops in the court, dark against the lit windows across the way. Plover leaned over and kissed her and she responded passionately. He put his hand on her breast and she pressed it tighter with her own hand. After a while, Plover removed the dog from the couch and he and Kolya lay together kissing and fondling each other. They did not talk at all until Plover tried to reach up under her dress.

"No," she said softly, but her tone meant no. Plover opened his eyes and moved his head. Her eyes were open, too.

"Why not?" he asked.

She struggled to sit up, and he helped her. "Look," she said, "I think we're going to end up in bed, but not to-night."

"Do you have any special reason?" Plover asked.

She smiled. "We barely know each other."

The next day, when Plover thought about it, it made sense. They were not going to have any casual fuck together. That wasn't what either of them wanted. This was to be more serious. This was to be an affair between friends, and they did not know each other yet well enough for that.

For some reason, he thought about Mollie, back at Gate Five. Mollie had been very nice to him, now that he looked back on it. He had needed a woman desperately, and she had come to him. She had not demanded that he take her out, buy her drinks, or even sit with her. She had simply let him haul her out of the bar and bed her. Of course you could say that Mollie was a cheap whore who would let almost anybody fuck her, but that would be missing the point even if it was true. The point was that she had made love to *him*. He told himself that when he got back to Sausalito he was going to be a lot nicer to Mollie. She was a nice person.

That night Plover and Kolya went to a movie and had a light supper afterward in a theatrical district restaurant with wood-paneled walls and framed caricatures. The food was good and the service excellent. Plover was always a little uncertain of himself in restaurants, but these waiters, both tonight and last night, had made him feel at ease; he was not quite sure how. Perhaps it was also this beautiful woman on his arm, who led without seeming to lead and who had eyes only for him.

When they got back to her place after walking the dog, Plover did not try to seduce her. They had their drinks on the couch and talked until four in the morning, and then with a final hot kiss he left her, letting himself out the front door onto the nearly icy street. It took him ten minutes to find a cab, but he was still warm from the touch of her mouth against his. It was remarkable. He wondered if he was falling in love.

On the next night he forced the issue. She invited him to have dinner at her place, steaks and salad, and when it was all over he said, "Tonight, we're going to bed." They were in the hallway between the kitchen and the living room. Plover had her pushed up against the wall, and before she could answer him he kissed her hard. For only a moment he feared she would say that they had to walk the dog, or that she could not, or that he was behaving badly, or anything that would stop them. But she did not. After the kiss she took him by the hand and led him upstairs.

23

Plover had never been on the second floor of her apartment before. It seemed very large, with a bathroom off the hall by the stairs, and at least three bedrooms that he could see. In the light from the hall he could see that one looked like a boy's bedroom, with what appeared to be a stuffed owl surrounded by small model airplanes on the bureau, as if the owl were under attack. But he did not have time to look closer. She led him by the hand into her own bedroom, which seemed all gray silk and dark wood, and while he watched her she stood in the middle of the lighted room and undressed, looking at him whenever possible. Finally she was white and naked. She sat on the edge of the bed and then lay back, her hands crossing her breasts, her eyes sparkling. Plover realized he was still dressed. He grinned, more from excitement than from amusement, and began to undress himself. She watched him without speaking. At last he joined her on the bed, his erect penis grazing her thigh as he moved over her and began to kiss her.

The feel of her skin against his was faintly moist. He wondered if he was sweating, and then knew he was. He could feel the sweat on his forehead. He was very much aware of what he was doing as he stopped kissing her on the mouth and moved down to kiss her breasts. Instead of getting more excited he got less excited, and he could feel his erection going away. That made him think about it all the more, which made it go away all the faster. At last she said, "What's the matter?" and he said grimly, "I don't know," and they rolled apart. Plover stared at the ceiling.

"There isn't any hurry," she said.

"I know." But time did not matter to him. He felt less like making love than he ever had in his life. He wondered if he would ever be able to make love to anyone but Thalia in his whole life. He did not count Mollie. He had been drunk with Mollie. And now that he pressed the issue, he was not sure he had actually fucked her. Very conveniently, he had blacked out. Probably after the fact. He wondered if in the morning he would be able to remember any of this. He was not drunk, but maybe he blacked out every time he had a fiasco. He certainly could not remember any others.

She was up on one elbow, looking down at him. Her hair was messy and lovely and her eyes still bright. "Don't brood," she said. "Just relax. We can use this time to get to know each other."

"You want to talk?" he said sarcastically.

"Not if you don't," she said.

"I want to fuck," he said, still sarcastic. "But it looks like that's out of the question."

"We can fuck later," she said. "When you're more relaxed. Do you want a beer?"

"That's right, I can't get it on without boozing up. Sure, by all means, gimme a beer." He thought about asking her to bring along her cigarettes, but stopped himself. Self-pity had to have limits. He was not going to start smoking again, just because he had fucked his last fuck. There were other things in life.

He watched her walk across the room and out the door, barefoot and naked. She had a lovely little body. Smaller than Thalia, with less tits but a better ass. Thalia. There she was again. That was the problem. Thalia was in the bedroom with them. Talk about three-way scenes!

He took hold of his little tiny penis, which seemed to be trying to retreat right up into his groin. He pressed his thumb into the head and released it, watching the whitened flesh turn purplish again. Lack of blood. He wondered where all the blood was. Back in his ass, hiding. He wondered what it was that had frightened his blood. Was it having the lights on? Was it the fact that she probably knew more about sex than he did, and he was subconsciously afraid of being corny? After all, she had been married four times, and had probably been to bed with a lot of guys. Plover had not had much experience when he got married, and almost none afterward, unless you counted Thalia. All those years together. They had fucked every possible way. He remembered once, on a

New Year's morning, when they had gone to a party and come home bloody drunk he had savagely fucked her in the ass, and she had just as savagely loved it. But they never did it again. He did not like to do things to her that gave him orgasm but gave her none. She had orgasms, yes. She was very good at having orgasms. So he always liked to be fucking her properly when he himself came, so that they could come together. He would eat her, or fuck her breasts, or her armpits, or crawl all over her just barely letting the tip of his penis brush against her skin, but when the final moment came he would plunge into her and they would go off together.

Sometimes. Other times he would get a hard-on, fuck her, and crawl off, not sure whether she made it or not, and not much caring.

And other times. When she wanted to fuck and he didn't. When he would pretend to be asleep, or ill, or anything to make her stop touching him. A lot of that, over the years. More of it than anything else. More of it, surely, than the wild nights.

Kolya entered the bedroom carrying a tray with two tall glasses of beer on it. She smiled at him. "Service for two, my lord and master." It was a weak attempt at humor, but Plover felt obliged to laugh. He moved back and propped himself up against the pillows, and she walked around the bed, put down the tray and joined him. They drank beer quietly for a few moments, and then Plover said, "I've been thinking about my wife."

"Ha, that's what they all say." She touched his hip with her fingertips, to take the sting out of the remark, and then left them there.

"I guess I was never really much good to her," he said, and abruptly Kolya sat up, almost spilling her beer.

"I don't want to hear that," she said. "You stop talking like that. You feel sorry for yourself and hate yourself a little bit because your wife left you. But don't bring that to me. I don't want to hear you putting yourself down. I like you. If I didn't like you a great deal, you wouldn't be in this bed and you know it. And if I like you, there must be something very good to like."

"I'm sorry," he said.

"I hope you don't think I let any man I go out with come to bed with me," she said.

"No, I don't think that," Plover said. He could not help thinking that it had taken him four nights to get here, and he wondered if that was average. So he did think she was *promiscuous*. What a word! "Hey, I'm really sorry. I guess I do have a Puritan conscience. Maybe that's what's the matter with me."

"Maybe you're just a little shy," she said. "For Christ's sake, don't be so tough on yourself. You're not fifteen years old anymore. You can't get an erection just by thinking pleasant thoughts. It takes a little time and patience."

He could not help saying, "You've had more experience with this sort of thing than I have."

She began to react, and then visibly calmed herself. "You're still very tense," she said. "Just sit back and relax, drink your beer," and she got up and turned out the lights and came back to the bed in the darkness. He could feel her take his penis in her fingers, and then felt her mouth close around it. He waited for it to come erect, but it did not. Finally, he stopped waiting and did what she had said to do—sat back and relaxed. He could feel sweat trickling down from his armpits, so he knew he was still nervous, but he stopped trying to analyze *why* he was nervous. He could feel parts of her body touching his legs, and her hair against his stomach, soft and pleasant-feeling. It was very nice to be blown like this, quietly and in the dark. He had a bottle of beer on the bedside table, and he could take a sip if he wanted to. Of course he did not want to. It would be too crude. She was very good at what she was doing, and gradually he could feel himself unlimber, and then get hard. Even so, he let it go on a long time because it was so peaceful just to lie back and do nothing. There was no hurry.

He came almost before he knew it, with mind-scattering intensity. He did not even have time to take hold of her. He lay back again, his head resting against the pillows, and opened his eyes. She was still down there, but he could feel her moving. She got up and went into the bathroom and closed the door. He heard water running. He felt pretty good, except for the fact that she had not had a chance to have an orgasm. That was too bad. But the fiasco problem had been met and conquered, that was something.

She came out of the bathroom and turned on the light. She was carrying a steaming washcloth, and while Plover continued to lie back, she washed off his genitals with the warm cloth. Plover pretended to have his eyes shut, but actually he was watching her. She seemed to love what she was doing, and a rush of emotion came over him: *This is really a good person,* he thought. It had never occurred to him before that a lover could be a good person, in just those words. He continued to squint at Kolya after she stopped what she was doing and sat up. He wondered what she was thinking about. He could not see her face. He reached out a hand and touched her at the small of the back. She turned toward him, her face calm and lovely, and then bent down to be kissed.

"You're really very nice," he said.

"Thank you."

They lay together, naked and cosy, talking until almost dawn, and then Plover fell asleep.

24

The next night they decided to go to bed early, and so they stayed home and watched television, holding hands. Plover drank a lot of beer and was heavily sleepy when they went upstairs at last. He did not expect to have the problem, but as soon as he was undressed he began to wonder and the wondering made him a bit nervous, and so when Kolya came out of the bathroom naked he was already under the bedcovers, his eyes shut. She turned off the light and climbed into bed with him. While they kissed she kneaded him with her fingers until he came erect, and he turned her over and began to mount her. The erection was weak, he felt, and he would have to do something with it right away, before it flagged. He penetrated her quickly and she gave a slight moan and dug her fingers into his back. He felt the weight of the covers on him and kicked with his legs. The covers would not loosen, and finally he had to throw them off with his arm, meanwhile staying inside her. At last he could concentrate on lovemaking, and he began pumping vigorously, so as to come before his erection vanished. He also wanted her to know that he was a fierce and violent lover. He growled and bit her shoulder and kissed her hard, squeezing her with his hands. He was nervous and tense, and he was not enjoying himself very much. He knew she was not having much fun, either, from the way she was responding. He could sense that she was not going to get there as quickly as himself, but instead of slowing down, he speeded up, and came in a series of jerky spasms. He tried to pretend he had not come, but she was not fooled. She stopped responding entirely, and so he quit, too, and pulled away from her, rolling over on his back.

For a while they did not speak, and then Kolya said, "What was the hurry?"

"I don't know what you mean," Plover said. He reached for her hand. "Of course I do. I'm sorry. Nerves, I guess."

"These things take time," she said.

25

The next night she took him to a Broadway play, and Plover discovered that he enjoyed dressing up and mingling with other dressed-up people. With Kolya to guide him he did not feel out of place or clumsy, and when she spotted some friends and they were asked to join a party for supper afterward, he did not feel frightened. He did not know why, any more than he knew why such things had frightened him in the past. The whole group moved to the wood-paneled restaurant Plover and Kolya had been to before, and it was nearly three before they got home, happy and drunk the both of them. Walking the dog was an adventure, and it was not until they got into bed, the lights still on, that they stopped giggling.

"Oops," Kolya said. "I forgot something."

"What?" Plover asked.

"You shouldn't ask a lady that kind of question at a moment like this," she said. "I have to get something, that's all."

"Ah, the famous pill," he said. "Don't go away just for a goddamn pill. You can take it later."

"I don't take pills. I don't believe in them. I have to get my diaphragm, if you must know."

He hugged her to him. "Not just yet," he said. "I feel so good. Let's just lie here." It was true. He felt sublime, lazily powerful and complete. Although he hardly bothered to think about it, he had an erection that seemed hard as a rock. But above all, he felt comfortable and did not want her to go away. They kissed and fondled each other, half awake—not even half awake, but deep down into an awakened sleep, a sensual half-dreamworld. Without even thinking, he began to mount her. "Please," she said. "Oh," he said, "I won't come. I promise. I just want to fuck for a while." She said nothing more, and he entered her slowly and easily. It seemed so nice to just lie quietly, moving only a little, stopping from time to time, kissing her ear, her eyes, and her hair, being very slow and gentle, not thinking about anything except how good it all felt.

Then he began to know what he was doing, and the pleasure increased. His goal was not to come, but to keep fucking forever, slowly and gently, but with more suppressed force than he had ever felt before. She was in exact tune with him, and he could feel her rising, a fraction at a time, toward her own climax; rising toward it so slowly that he could afford to take all the time he wanted; and he wanted forever. He had never felt anything like this in his life. It was not mindless. He knew exactly what he was doing. His sense of time was not distorted, and his other senses were all functioning properly. It was as if the rules of sexual intercourse had been suspended temporarily, and he could continue to increase the pleasure and excitement infinitely without coming. Without actually coming. Because he felt that he was coming-without-coming right now, and had felt that way for at least an hour. Yes, he had been fucking her—they had been fucking—for over an hour, and she was moaning now, her body moving slightly from side-to-side. He thought, all I have to do is increase the speed slightly, just slightly, and I can make her come. But he did not want to, and so perversely he slowed down even more, just barely moving, and felt her respond trembling as if her body was trying to merge with his. This was very funny, and within himself he laughed at the idea of their bodies merging. That was not what was happening. What was happening was that their sex organs were filling the universe, and the two of them were lost inside it, happy to be lost, in an infinite sea of warmth and love.

But then something happened, and he could sense a change in her, a difference in her trembling and in the way she clung to him and moved. There was a difference in the sounds she was making and in the look in her eyes, as he rose back to look at her. He smiled down at her and began to move just slightly faster. It registered in her eyes like an electric shock, and her mouth began to make sounds he could not at first hear, and then recognized as words: "Oh, God, oh Christ, oh my God," over and over, louder each time until her whole body became a vise to clench him and she screamed with delight and release.

They lay together a long time before he withdrew his still hard, still unexpended erection. "Didn't you come?" she asked.

He laughed, still terribly excited, still lost in the delight of what had happened, and what was still happening. "Not yet," he said. "I promised, remember?" She put her arms around his neck and pulled herself up to kiss him softly on the mouth. "You just wait a minute," she said. She got out of bed and he lay back dreamily, not exactly waiting, still suspended in his senses, until she returned and got up on top of him and slid herself down on his penis. "You just lie there," she said.

"Can I come this time, teacher?" he said. She giggled at him and began to rock gently. After a while he felt himself moving toward orgasm, and he decided to do something he had never done before: he would be looking into her eyes as he came. He opened his eyes to look at her. Her eyes were shut and her arms were held out, as if she was dancing to a slow tune. He touched her hip and said, "Look at me." She opened her eyes and he put both his hands lightly on her hips and they watched each other as first he came and then, more gently, she came for the second time. Afterward he could hardly believe that it had all happened. By the clock they had been making love just a little over four hours, but it had seemed like days. He had not believed himself capable of such magnificent lovemaking, and he was not ashamed to call it and himself magnificent, because that was what it was.

26

When Plover got back to Jack Raiford's apartment the telephone was ringing. He wondered whether to answer it or not. But of course he did; he could not just stand there and let the thing go on ringing. His skin began to go tight as he heard the operator telling him that it was a person-to-person call for Mr. Franklin Plover from Mrs. Plover.

"This is me," he said.

"Frank?"

"Yes, Honey. Hello." The telephone was on a small table next to Jack's easy chair, and Plover sat down slowly, leaning backward to adjust the Venetian blinds. The apartment smelled musty and unused. There was faint crackling over the telephone line. Thalia said, "I just thought I'd call and see how you were getting along." She paused, and he said nothing. Then she said, "The children would like to say hello, too."

"I was going to call," he said.

"It's Sunday," she said. "The rates are lower."

"Yeah, I was going to call later on. How are you?"

"We're all fine. I took the girls swimming yesterday. It's been good and hot here."

"You wouldn't believe New York weather. Whew. What shit."

"Have you had any luck getting a job?"

"I haven't actually been looking much. Jack's out of town. Down in Washington like a hotshot. In fact, I haven't even watched the news to see if he's on. Some house guest, huh?"

Thalia laughed. There was another long pause between them, and she said, "Do you want to speak to the girls?"

"Yeah, put them on," he said. Each of the girls talked to him for a minute or so, and then he asked to speak to Thalia again. "Honey? How *are* you?"

"I'm better," she said. She sounded better.

"I think you were right. We needed this time away from each other. It's going to do us a lot of good. We'll be able to talk about things without all that goddamn pressure on us."

"Are you really thinking of moving to New York? Do you like it there?"

"It's beautiful. It's one of the most beautiful cities in the world. Probably *the* most beautiful city in the world. Some of the people are the nicest and most beautiful, too. But the rest are maniacs. I wouldn't live here for a mil-

155

lion dollars a year." As soon as he said it he knew it was true. "But I'm glad for the visit."

"You're not really looking, then," she said.

"No. I've been playing tourist. I'll never leave the Bay Area. It's my *home*."

"Do you know when you'll be coming back?"

"Well, I said a month. I guess it'll have to be a month. There are some things I want to look into, professionally. Not a move but maybe a change. I can't really talk about it because it isn't anything yet."

"I understand," she said.

"Well, I guess this is starting to cost money," he said. He was very careful not to say, "I love you," although he wanted very much to. But things were teetering on a balance, he could tell, and he did not want to do or say anything that would tip it the wrong way. They managed a clumsy farewell, and he hung up. His hand was sweating against the receiver, and he wiped it on the fabric of the chair. Strangely, he did not feel guilty about having just come from Kolya. That had been too beautiful an experience to be sullied with guilt; when he and Thalia got back on the track and started really trying to find out what had gone wrong and how to fix it, it was the kind of thing that he could tell her about. Not right away, but later, after he and she had managed to have that kind of sexual experience between themselves.

Because there could be no mistake. Thalia was opening groundwork for a reconciliation. Why else would she have called? It was working. The separation was actually working. Given enough time by herself to think things out, she had seen her actions in their true light. Of course it would not be easy for either of them, particularly her, to go back after all that had happened. Gentleness, forgiveness, and kindness would have to be the way; and a real attempt on his part to understand himself and to correct his flaws.

27

For most of the rest of his time in New York, Plover slept days in Jack Raiford's apartment, getting up at around three or four in the afternoon. He would dress and walk down to Ninth Avenue for copies of the *New York Times* and the *Post*, which he would take back to the apartment to read over breakfast and in the bathroom. Then he would take a nice hot shower, dress, and catch a cab across town to Third and 47th Street, where he would meet Kolya. She worked as an editor for Harcourt, and he would either wait for her in the bookstore on the street level or outside on one of the marble benches. She was never more than a few minutes late, and after the first few times he met her and wished he had kissed her when she first came out of the building, he began to do so, in front of all the other people. He did not care, and neither did she.

During the day she would have decided what they were going to do that evening: a play, a movie, a cocktail party, or, more often than anything else, dinner alone together. Over dinner they talked about everything. He had never done this with Thalia and he bitterly regretted it; but he knew that when they got back together their lives were going to be different, and they were going to have more *romance*. In a way, he looked on his affair with Kolya as an education in romance. Not that he was so cold-blooded about it; he loved Kolya, and told her so all the time. He did not love Thalia any the less, he told her; it was just that now he loved two women.

After dinner they would walk or take a cab to the Village and Kolya's apartment. She thought it was extravagant to take taxis all the time, but he would not go down into the subway. Once after he had picked her up after work she had wheedled him into the subway at rush hour, and after they had gotten down into it she had begun to laugh and walk fast between the commuters and subway riders, dodging in and out and almost losing Plover. He was not used to it and he did not know how to either dodge or shove. For some reason he did not see the humor in it, and when Kolya finally stopped and let him catch up, he shoved his face into hers and said between his teeth, "God damn you, don't do that again!" They patched up the quarrel over dinner, when Plover explained that he had a slight fear of crowds, and she never asked him to use the subway again.

They would walk the dog and then settle down cosily in the living room, Plover with his glass of beer and

Kolya with a brandy, until it was time to go to bed. Although Kolya was due at work between nine-thirty and ten in the morning, she never seemed to want to go to sleep. If they were not making love they were talking, often about making love, and again Plover resolved that he would bring this new pleasure back to Thalia, too, and they would begin to share new intimacies.

They did not repeat that remarkable four-hour love-making episode. They did not even try. But Plover had no more trouble having erections, and Kolya, once she was able to relax with him, had no difficulty in having one or more orgasms each night. She had admitted to him, "I almost never come the first time with a man."

"It's funny," Plover said "I never think of women as being shy, just like guys. You always think the girl is either frigid or not frigid. Never anything in between."

Another surprise for Plover was that he was not jealous of her earlier husbands and lovers. Thalia had been a virgin when Plover married her, and the thought, even the fantasy, that another man might touch her sent Plover into a wracking jealousy. But not with Kolya. Somehow it did not seem to matter as much, as if the knowledge that this was an affair and would end soon suspended the rules. There simply was not time for fights, jealousy, envy, spite, or any of the other traditional emotional difficulties.

Kolya talked quite freely about her lovers and husbands, so freely that Plover finally understood that she would one day talk just as freely about him. It was an odd feeling, not entirely unpleasant.

Jack Raiford was amused by the whole thing. He had come back from Washington to find Plover shifty-eyed and murmuring excuses why he could not go out and get drunk with him. Plover finally admitted to Jack that he and Thalia had broken up and that he had come to New York looking for a job.

"God, you and *Thalia?* I can't believe it!" was Raiford's reaction. But after he told Plover how sorry he was about the whole situation, he said, "Listen, getting you a job here shouldn't be too difficult. I'll get you a couple of appointments for tomorrow morning. . . ."

"I don't want an appointment," Plover said.

"Why not? What the hell *did* you come to New York for? Don't you want a job?"

Now it was really getting sticky. "Uh, I changed my mind." He was not going to mention his feeling that Thalia was changing hers. Word magic or anything you want to call it, he was not going to say anything to anybody.

"Listen, I would have no trouble at all getting you on the staff," Raiford said. "This is the big time, baby. Tough, mean, and cruel. But big time means big rewards, and I do mean liquor, dames, and dough. Get the message?"

"I guess I can't hack it," Plover said. He did not even want to make jokes about it. Raiford finally gave up on him and they shared the apartment without seeing each other more than a few times. Plover was sure that Raiford was contemptuous of him for shying away from New York, but Raiford never said anything of the kind, and in fact, when he drove Plover to Kennedy Airport he said, "God damn, I got to envy you, going back to that beautiful city," and he sounded as if he meant it.

Plover talked to Thalia and the children twice more

before flying home, and he was very careful to say nothing that would force Thalia to back away from him. He was polite, interested in what she was saying, and never pushy about learning what was going on with her. The phone calls left him nervous and tense for a few minutes, but always he regained his good spirits and always he regained his optimism about the future.

28

Shortly before he left New York Plover learned that Kolya was engaged to be married and that her fiancé had probably had them followed. They had left the Harcourt Building and gone west a couple of blocks and then turned north. There was plenty of pedestrian traffic, and they moved along, arm-in-arm with the crowd, but at each corner, because they were not quite sure where they were going, they missed the light and had to wait for the next one. Plover noticed after the third time that a man in a light tan raincoat was also missing the lights and crossing with them, although he always stood back, rather than right on the curb. At the next light Plover said to Kolya, "Wait a minute. Are you sure you want to keep going uptown? Why don't we go over to Fifth?" She laughed. This had been their argument all along. He held her arm and they waited for the light to change again. Plover was certain the man had waited, too, but he did not turn to look. Sure enough, when they crossed the street the man passed them and walked on ahead. In the middle of the next block the man stopped, as if to look in a window, and Plover and Kolya passed him. Plover did not turn around to check if the man was still following. By now he was certain of it, a little afraid, and also a little excited. After all, he was ahead of the man, whoever he was. Plover knew the man was following them, and the man did not know Plover knew.

"Don't look around," he said to Kolya, "but we're being tailed."

"What?"

"Don't look around. But remember the guy in the tan raincoat who's been hitting the traffic lights the same as us?"

"No. Frankly—"

"Now, wait a minute. I'll prove it to you. Next corner we turn left, and then I'll pull you into a store front. We'll be looking at something in the window. When we come out, look around. You'll see a guy, young, maybe twenty-five, slim, maybe a light-skinned Negro, wearing a tan raincoat. He'll be hanging around waiting for us."

Kolya laughed. He loved the sound of her laugh, and it made him feel light-headed, to have an affair in New York City and be followed, probably by a detective. After all, a nut would have approached them, or looked screwy, or something. Plover remembered something from his readings of detective stories: "Listen, when we come out of the doorway, look the bastard right in the eye. That'll put him off."

So at the next corner they turned and walked west again, and after a few stores, Plover pulled them into the entryway of a camera shop, and stared at the camera equipment in the window. When they came out, the man in the tan raincoat was standing at the curb, as if waiting for a cab. Plover, filled with delightful daring, said, "Hey, buddy!" and the man turned toward them. "Gotcha!" Plover said. The man looked surprised, and then turned away and began to cross the street. To Plover there was something about the set of the man's shoulders that indicated defeat.

They decided to take a cab to her place instead of stopping for a cocktail. Kolya couldn't remember where the place she wanted to go was anyway. In the back of the cab, Plover said, "Well, were we or were we not being followed by that guy?"

"Oh, I don't think so," Kolya said. "Why would anybody want to follow us?"

"Well, it couldn't be the FBI, because they don't employ Negros, except to wash cars. So he must be a private eye. And I'm new to town, so he must be following you."

She turned and looked at him. "You sound happy. Why would being followed make you happy?"

"I'm happy because of you," he said. "And it's an adventure. What the hell, baby, and all that stuff. Do you have any guilty secrets? I mean, can you figure out who would want to have you tailed?"

At her place Plover walked the dog while she showered and changed, and then they went to a bar called the

Lion's Head for a cup of coffee. Plover held her hand shamelessly on top of the table. He did not ask her any more questions about being followed. While he had been walking the dog he thought about it and decided that she would tell him if she wanted to and would not if she didn't. Anyway it was a great deal of fun, and he would not have missed it for anything.

While they were drinking their coffee and it turned dark outside, she told him she was engaged to marry a man in the clothing business. He was in Los Angeles on business and wouldn't be back for another three weeks. By that time Plover would be gone. She had not seen any reason to bring it up. "I didn't mean to fall in love with you," she said. "And once I had, it didn't make any difference."

Plover wanted to know all about him, and so they had another cup of coffee, and she told him that her fiancé was in his late fifties, had three children of his own, in their teens, and that she wanted some security. He was moderately wealthy and he loved her. His name was Solomon Wientraub, and she called him Solly. Plover had an image of him: small, delicate, a sweet expression of wisdom and humor. This was not the case, however. Kolya had a photograph of him in her purse and she showed it to Plover. He saw a man at least six feet tall (in the photo he was standing next to Kolya, and they were both posed stiffly in bathing suits, his hand on her arm) with dark eyes and dark hair, handsome in an almost ruthless way, and looking nowhere near fifty. "Jesus," Plover said. He handed back the photograph. "You think it was him having us followed?"

"Who else could it be?" she said. "Although I'm still not certain anybody was following us."

Plover did not try to convince her. He was morally certain and now he was slightly afraid, too. What if the guy, *Solly,* decided to come home and take care of matters? Plover had read about the gangster epoch in American history, and he knew all about Murder, Inc., and the goons of the garment industry. He had a quick picture of himself sliced to pieces and lying dead in an alley. He looked across the table at Kolya.

"What are you thinking?" she asked him.

He burst out laughing, so loud that people at other tables looked at him. "Never mind," he said.

29

And then one night she told him that two of her children were returning from their visit with their father, and that the affair was ended. The children would be back the next day. And so this was their last night. It caught Plover by surprise. Somehow he had not expected it to happen at all. They would go on like this, having the best of everything. But of course not. It would end, and it would end tomorrow. No, tonight. He could not stay the night. What if the children were brought in to find him there? No. He would have to leave early, some time during the night. He felt his skin growing waxen. They were sitting on a bench in Washington Square, and pretty soon they were going down to Little Italy for some food.

Plover wanted a cigarette very badly, and to make the urge go away, he began breathing deeply.

"What's wrong?" she asked. "We knew it had to end."

"You don't have to be so cold-blooded about it," he said. "Oh, Christ, I know, you women can do any goddamn thing you please. Men are the weak ones. Oh, Christ."

"I didn't want you thinking about it, that's all," she said. "It wouldn't help. I'm sorry."

Plover was sullen and upset all through dinner. He did not like the restaurant, for one thing. It was in a basement, and there were food stains on the checkered blue and white tablecloths. Instead of a salad, they were given a large platter of antipasto which looked as if it had been left around for days. The salami was stringy and the carrots were mushy and tasteless. The spaghetti stuck together and the sauce was thin and lukewarm. Altogether it was a grim experience, and for the first time over a meal, Plover and Kolya did not talk. Most of the other guests in the restaurant seemed to be Italian, and Plover imagined he could smell their combined garlic breaths. Still, he ate doggedly and drank the sourish red wine and hoped Kolya was well aware of how he felt. He was in no mood for self-sacrifice. She, on the other hand, seemed to be perfectly content with her food. Maybe New Yorkers didn't know any better. Maybe they thought this was quaint and ethnic.

He was still in shock. The affair was over and he was going to have to go home and muddle through a reconciliation with Thalia. He felt a pang of guilt. Almost as if, in his present mood, he really did not want a reconciliation. But that was nonsense, and he felt better just from telling himself it was nonsense. He looked across at Kolya. She was not as beautiful as he had once thought. For one thing, the flanges of her nose were a little too wide. And there were fine wrinkles on her neck.

She looked up and caught him staring at her. She stopped chewing and said, "Are you still mad at me?"

"I was just noticing how beautiful you are," he said, half-kidding himself and half-kidding her. But the way her eyes looked when he said it changed his mood entirely. She lay down her fork and reached across the table to touch his hand. "I'm so sorry," she said.

A feeling of warmth began seeping through Plover as if someone had given him a shot of morphine. That was the only thing he could think of to compare it to. From his sour mood of only a few seconds ago he felt himself changed into a warm and loving man.

Never mind that the affair was going to end. He was with her now and he loved her, and the feeling—the delicious warm feeling—came from being with her. Nothing could hurt him. Time was not passing. He felt perfect. He tried to explain it to her, and after she got over being pleased that he was no longer in a bad mood, she began herself to feel the same way, or so she told him, and they drifted hand-in-hand out of the restaurant and up to the street. They walked to her apartment through the muggy night and after once more walking the dog, he kissed her good-bye and did not go back upstairs.

30

There was a mixup at the airport. Plover waited for Thalia at the passenger gate, and Thalia waited for Plover at the baggage pickup. When Plover finally showed up to claim his baggage he was red-faced and angry. He had assumed that Thalia had either stood him up or was up to her usual old trick of never being anywhere on time. She, on the other hand, had been afraid he had missed the plane. When he saw her standing by herself in the long low baggage room his first thought was, "Jesus Christ! I'll bet she's been here all the time!" He tried to make himself smile at her, but the burst of irritation was too pleasureful to resist: "God damn, I've been waiting for you half an hour!"

It was not a good way to begin a reconciliation, but as

it turned out, there was no reconciliation to begin. Plover had been kidding himself, and Thalia had merely been trying to be pleasant on the telephone. She had not changed her mind at all. After he got his bags and they started their walk down under the street and across to the parking garage, he said, "Thale, I'm sorry about yelling at you. The trip anxiety really gets to me."

"How was New York?" she asked.

"What's more important, how are *you*?" he asked.

"I'm all right. Do you know where you'll be staying? Are you going back to Tony's?"

He had not even thought about it. Somehow his mind had allowed him to believe that he was going home. Even if there was going to be a reconciliation (he did not know yet that there was not) he would still have to stay someplace until she actually melted and asked him home. "Gee," he said. "I guess I'll *have* to stay at Tony's. I didn't call him or anything."

At the car she gave him his key and he got in on the driver's side. After she got in and settled he turned toward her, wanting to kiss her. She seemed to understand this, because she looked embarrassed and turned away from him.

"Nothing's changed," she murmured.

"What did you say?"

She faced him. "Nothing's changed. I just wanted to tell you."

"Oh, God," he said.

"I'm sorry. I thought if I had time to myself it would help me think things through, but I haven't even had the time. I've been so busy and my mind's been so rattled, I just don't know. I do know nothing's changed, though."

172

"Yeah, that would be the one thing you'd be sure of."

After a while he started the car and they drove through the labyrinth to the exit. Plover paid fifty cents to the collector and they drove out into the sunshine.

"See, I can pay money and all that stuff," he said. He wanted to stop the car and cry, but he would not give her the satisfaction. He wondered where he was driving to. Not Tony's. He could not just gather his bags and say good-bye to her. It was his car. He would have to drive her home. He did not want to see the house or the children; he did not think he could face it. He would break down and cry. He did not want to cry. He had done all the crying he ever wanted to do.

But there was no choice for him. It was as if he had never gone to New York at all. All the same feelings were in place, and he had gained nothing. He pulled off the freeway at the San Bruno exit and made the loop and drove over the freeway and then off the road. By this time he could barely see, and Thalia was asking him what was the matter.

"Nothing," he said, but his voice rose. "Aw, fuck it!" he squeaked, and got out of the car. There were some acacia trees beside the shoulder, and he went and stood among them. He cried and bellowed, and his eyes and nose ran, and finally he was finished. He did not have a handkerchief, and so he had to get back into the car looking awful and sniffling. He used a couple of Kleenex from the glove compartment. Thalia sat stiffly, looking straight ahead. "I'm all right now," he said.

"I'm sorry," she said.

"It's not your fault. I built the whole thing up in my imagination."

He started the car and they drove through San Bruno to the freeway.

"It is my fault, in a way," she said, "because Jackie told me about this."

"Who's Jackie?" Plover said. They did not know any Jackies.

"She's a friend of mine," Thalia said with strong emphasis on the word friend. "She told me you might have thought there would be a change in me. But I didn't believe her, because we didn't say anything on the telephone."

Plover did not like the idea of this Jackie interfering in their private lives. "Who is she?" he asked.

"I told you. She's a friend of mine. I met her in art class."

"Art class?"

"I'm taking art. I told you that."

"No you did not."

"Well I meant to."

"Anyway. Jackie."

"She's been divorced. She was in your position. She didn't want the divorce. She's been a great help. She's been telling me how it feels from that position. I understand how you must feel much better now," she said.

"I don't think you do," Plover said stiffly.

"Well, she was right about the way you'd react today."

To Plover this meant that from now on he would be measured very carefully by Thalia against a standard of conduct set up by this Jackie person, whom he already hated. He particularly did not like Thalia running around with a divorced woman. And *art* class! Why in the name of Christ would she be wasting his money on art class?

"What's art class like?" he asked her after a long silence.

"We're learning to make candles," she said. There was another long silence.

"Tell me about your friend," he said. It occurred to him that Thalia did not have many friends. In fact, if you took away *his* friends, she did not have any at all. One of the things he loved about her was that she was not interested in the typical suburban bullshit of kaffee klatches and bridge games and shopping sprees. In the time they had lived in Mill Valley they hadn't gotten to know a single neighbor.

"She's just a friend of mine, that's all," Thalia said. She sounded defensive and angry.

"What's the matter?"

"Nothing."

"Come on. Something must be the matter."

She turned toward him and he saw wetness in her eyes. "Don't you know how hard this is on me, too?" she said before she too broke down finally and sobbed.

31

Plover barely recognized his own house. Most of the furniture had been moved around and the rest of it was missing. There seemed to be candlewax dripped onto everything, and the smell of cat shit now had to compete with the smell of incense and scented candles. The place appeared to have been turned overnight into a hippie pad. Plover immediately suspected the influence of Jackie.

He kissed and hugged his children, and they took him into their room to see how it had been redecorated. He made the appropriate remarks as they showed him the new beds and desks and rugs and posters, thinking to himself that he was not made of money and this sort of thing would have to change, and then he went to the bathroom, also redecorated and full of strange-looking candles, and then impulsively he peeked into Thalia's bedroom. It, too, had been redecorated, but it was clean and neat, lovely in fact, all in soft pinks and grays and greens. It smelled faintly of perfume. It was a bedroom calculated to attract and then excite men. It made Plover sick. Back in the living room he hugged the children and promised to call them soon and told Thalia, who was in the kitchen making coffee, that he had to run and thanked her for picking him up and got out of there. He did not feel like crying. He was too sick for that.

As he drove back to Sausalito he realized just how fully he had been excluded from Thalia's life in the month he had been gone. There would be no going back now. He did not even want to go back. He did not want to live in that house with her. If this was the way she wanted to live, then they were farther apart than he had dreamed. It had probably been going on for years, she dominated by him and struggling to live with it, and he blind to it and thinking she was content.

He drove past Gate Five and on to the studio. He did not want to show up at Tony's with his baggage, as if he had expected Tony to invite him back. But after he parked in the lot and got his bags out of the car and carried them up the steps to the back door, he discovered that there was a brand-new shiny lock on the door, and his key would not fit it. It was Sunday and no one was inside. Plover got back in his car and drove down toward the heart of town. He could not shake the notion that the locks had been changed to keep him out. Of course that was impossible, but in his present mood he allowed himself to believe it. It was just perfect. The Old Town Saloon was crowded with the usual Sunday sailors and tourists. Tony was in place behind the service bar, busy with Ramos fizzes. He finally looked up and saw Plover. Was there a momentary flicker of irritation before he grinned and winked at Plover?

"There are a lot of things I have to tell you," he yelled at Plover. "I get off at seven. Meet me at the boat."

It was a nice sunny afternoon, and Gate Five looked cheerful. The ground was hardened into ruts, dusty and covered with broken glass, rocks, and papers, but Plover liked it better than the mud of winter. He carried his suitcases out the pier past several sleeping dogs. A couple of young men with their shirts off were hammering shingles onto the roof of a houseboat, and they waved at Plover as he went by. He grinned and said hello, and for a few minutes he felt as if he had actually come home.

He teetered down the chickenwalk to the landing beside Tony's boat, and was about to step aboard when the door opened and Peggy Lavan, wearing a brilliant emerald satin robe, stepped blinking into the sunlight.

"Oh, it's you. How was New York?" she asked him.

"Just great," he said. He stood there on the gently rocking landing, holding his suitcases.

"When did you get back?" she said. She did not move out of the doorway or do anything else that would make things any easier for Plover. She just stood there and smiled into the afternoon light.

"Oh, just this afternoon," he said. This was getting silly. She knew what he was doing standing there with the suitcases. It was her place to invite him in. Obviously, she was living there now. Plover had known she and Tony were friends. In fact, he had introduced them, now that he remembered. "Tony said to meet him here," Plover said.

"He's at work. He works until seven."

"I know. I just came from the bar."

"Well, come on in," she said, but she did not move.

"Say, how come there's a new lock on the back door at the station?"

She laughed. "Oh. Somebody busted in. Probably a junkie. So they changed the locks. Brilliant, huh?"

"I didn't want to leave these in the car," Plover said. He lifted his suitcases slightly. His arms were getting tired. "Junkies abound." It seemed to be a graceful way to get out of what had been a nearly impossible situation, and she showed her appreciation by saying, "Oh, come in and have a cup of coffee,"—this time really meaning it—and he did.

Later that afternoon he checked into a motel halfway between Mill Valley and Sausalito, stowed his suitcases, which he now hated the sight of, and went back to the Old Town Saloon. By midnight he considered himself drunk enough to go back to the motel and to sleep.

32

The summer deepened. Fog and tourists poured over the western hills into Sausalito, and Plover's life once more settled into a groove, although it was not a groove he particularly wanted to settle into. He lived in a motel—not the first one he had registered in, but another one closer to Sausalito with slightly larger rooms and slightly thicker walls—and worked at Station KLA three hours a day, five days a week. Lanny Dalrymple, the kid who had replaced him while he had been in New York, was put back to work as a rock disk jockey on the early evening shift, where he grumbled and looked sullen for three weeks and then quit and went to Los Angeles. Plover was glad to see him go. Lanny and Plover were the two who knew how easy his job was, and now only Plover knew it.

Yet it was not as easy as it had been. In the past several weeks a good deal of Plover's blandness had been rubbed away, and he was no longer able to shrug off a morning of talking to paranoids and imbeciles quite so easily. It was not quite as easy to dismiss callers with quips, and Plover felt that his show was no longer as entertaining as it had been. He decided he was probably slipping in the ratings. He had never actually believed the rating services, and now he was sure that his audience was dwindling and the services were missing it. One day he would come to work and Fiedler would have a new rating that showed Plover to have almost no audience at all. Then he would be eased out of his job and have to go back to being a disk jockey.

He had far too much time on his hands. He tried to fill the time in several ways. He made up a schedule for himself that included one hour per day househunting, one hour of strenuous physical exercise, four hours of reading —mostly history and current events (he had always wanted to get more of an education in history and current events)—and one hour for meditation. The rest of his day could be used for personal pleasures such as eating, drinking, and having company. Not at the motel, of course, but at the Old Town Saloon, where he became one of the most regular of the regulars.

The rest of the schedule went to pieces. Househunting was physical exercise enough, and after only a few days he quit again, shutting his mind off to the fact that he could not continue living in a motel at sixteen dollars a day. Once he went to the Mill Valley public library and browsed for nearly an hour, checking out a history of the French republics, a biography of William Randolph

Hearst, and a collection of pieces by A. J. Liebling, and eventually he managed to read them, but not before he had run up library fines of nearly five dollars.

Although the fog came over the hills nearly every day, it seldom got as far down as the yacht harbors and the houseboat areas, and Plover found himself spending quite a bit of time on the waterfront, wandering around with his hands in his pockets, watching people with their boats, or driving up to Gate Five or Six and hanging around with friends who had houseboats, especially Tony and Peggy Lavan. Once it was clear to everybody that Plover was looking for a place to live and was not going to ask if he could move back in with Tony they all relaxed and were good friends again. Peggy was a good cook, and often she and Tony asked Plover to share dinner with them. For Tony this was heaven. He had never enjoyed eating in restaurants, and to be able to come home and find a nice sexy woman, plenty of marijuana, and all the food he could eat was pure paradise. He kept telling Plover that he should find a woman. That would solve everything. He could move in with the woman and have things just as good as Tony.

Peggy knew better. "There's a period of mourning," she told them both. Peggy had never been married, but she had been in love plenty of times and hurt plenty of times. She had also done quite a bit of the hurting. Plover remembered one lovesick record company executive who kept hanging around the station for weeks, on one excuse or another, a little short man with almost no hair, who dressed in four-hundred-dollar leather suits and silk shirts. Peggy had spent a weekend with him in Big Sur and now he was ready to leave his wife and children for her. "Fuck off," was all she had for him, and eventually he did.

Plover also got into the habit of dropping in on Captain Poontang, whose real name was Lew Wetzel. Captain Poontang's houseboat was on the south side of Gate Five, more or less the slum area of the houseboat colony. "Even in this self-made ghetto, there's a wrong side to the tracks," Captain Poontang said to Plover. His boat was not tethered to a boardwalk, like Tony's but attached by rotting ropes to an old abandoned ferryboat buried in the mud. Dozens of small jerry-built boats were tied up to the back of the ferry, and crazy walkways led from the rotting fantail up over sunken boats to the newer boats farther out in the water; and out from that there were many boats that were simply anchored, and did not touch dry land at all.

Captain Poontang and his orange cat, Thomas P. Wetherby, lived aboard a converted navy 32-foot lifeboat on which a hut had been built. Inside the boat it was dark and smelled of cat shit and human sweat, but on top of the housing was a flat deck and some old rotting cane chairs. It was quite pleasant to sit out here and watch the activities of the area. The cat, Thomas P. Wetherby, had such a fancy name because he had once been a subscriber to Pacific Telephone and Telegraph. When Captain Poontang had been Lew Wetzel and had lived in New York, the cat had had no name, and had spent the first two years of its life in Lew's Village apartment. When Lew had decided to come west and break with society, he brought the cat along with him, and when the telephone company cut off Lew's service, Lew promptly sold his boat to Mr. Thomas P. Wetherby, an oil company executive just back from the Middle East. That, at any rate, was the story Lew gave to the telephone company service representative. When the installer came around to restore service Lew turned him on and gave him some pieces of hashish to take home. The cat never paid his telephone bill, either, and eventually the installer had to come back and regretfully disconnect service for the last time.

Captain Poontang got his nickname from the fact that he was very interested in girls. "There is no such thing as a bad fuck," he was fond of saying. "Only bad fuckers." For many years he had been a taxi driver in New York City, hanging around Times Square when he was off duty, wearing sharp clothes and trying to find ways to meet the best broads on Broadway, make a big score, and be seen with the right people. One day, for Plover's entertainment, he went down into his houseboat and rummaged around for a while, coming up with some snapshots taken over the years. One showed Lew Wetzel and a couple of other sharpies wearing zoot suits, arms over each other's shoulders, grinning slyly at the camera. The zoot suits were not the exaggerated Hollywood versions, but the real thing, one-button roll, wide-brimmed hat, pegged pants, and no keychain. The picture had been taken in 1943 or 1944, Lew was not sure which.

"Didn't you have to go in the service?" Plover asked, after looking over the photos.

"Naw. They thought a glass eye was some kind of a handicap," he said. He smiled impishly at Plover while Plover reacted.

"Glass eye?" he said, but as he said it, he could see that Lew's left eye was a fake. It was not conspicuous in any way, but now that he looked closely, the iris was not closed down against the brightness of the sunlight as it should have been and as the right eye was. He immediately stopped looking into the left eye and started looking into the right. He had not realized it before, but he habitually looked into peoples' left eyes when he was talking to them. It took a conscious effort to track the right eye instead.

"Didn't the cab company object?" he asked.

With that same characteristic satyr's smile, Lew said, "Them I didn't tell."

On another sunny afternoon Plover asked Captain Poontang what had finally uprooted him from New York. Lew stroked his long stringy beard and smiled. "I really don't know," he said. "I wish I did. Whatever it was, God bless it. New York is a gorgeous place, but I wouldn't want to live there more than forty years. Hah hah."

Lew had not restricted himself to the Times Square area. His apartment was on Perry Street in the Village, and he hung around the coffeehouses after they had begun to proliferate in the late fifties. "There's no better place to lurk, except maybe outside a high school. And the high schools have drawbacks, in the form of police and teachers. No such drawbacks in the coffeehouses. The girls who show up are mostly looking to be raped."

He had also spent a great deal of time in the public library on 42nd Street, educating himself, and like many self-educated men, Plover noticed, he knew a great deal about many things, but he had very little depth in any but a few subjects. In Lew's case, his depth was in Judaism and leftist thought. He also knew a great deal about gangsterism, but he had read none of the books on the subject. Plover was fascinated by this because he himself was a student of crime and had read all the books. Lew saw it from a different perspective: his father had been a furrier in New York during the entire period of the rackets and gangsterism, and Lew grew up hearing intimate stories about Lepke, Gurrah Jake, and the others. For many afternoons and early evenings, Plover, Captain Poontang, and Thomas P. Wetherby would sit on top of the houseboat talking about gangsters, Plover and Poontang passing the pipe back and forth and watching the twilight fog pour stoned over the commuter clogged freeway.

Anyway, one day Lew Wetzel sold his taxi medallion, bought a used car, piled his cat and possessions into it, and headed west, landing finally at Gate Five, where he sold the car, bought his boat and became Captain Poontang. "This is it," he said.

"You mean you'll live here until you die?" Plover asked.

Poontang arched one eyebrow dramatically at Plover and did not answer for a couple of minutes. Then: "I don't plan *anything*."

Clearly, the implication was that planning was wrong. Plover was not sure he agreed. He was still enough the father and husband to feel a twist in his guts at the thought of going through life unplanned. He could see where it would be all right for people like Poontang and the other dropouts who lived in Gate Five, but not for himself. One thing both fascinated and worried him about Poontang. He did not want to ask for fear of seeming to be a square, but he wondered how Poontang stayed alive. What he ate on. At first he thought Poontang was a dope dealer, and it irritated him, but eventually he discovered that although there was almost no drug Poontang would not take, except cocaine, he was definitely not a dealer. He had nothing against dealers, he simply was not one of them. "They get a bad press," he said. "In some cases they're like angels of mercy, but they always get bad-mouthed in the press."

"What about when they turn on little kids?" Plover asked.

"They don't turn on little kids," Poontang said scornfully. "Little kids turn each other on. Teenypushers, hah hah."

"Yeah, but they get the dope from dealers, don't they?"

"Of course."

"Then it's the same thing, isn't it?"

"Maybe." He did not want to discuss it any more. Plover gradually came to learn that Captain Poontang held many romantic ideas about underworld figures and occupations, especially dealers and rapists, which would not bear deeper investigation. Poontang loved to talk about raping twelve-year-old girls, a thing which drove Plover half insane, since he happened to have a twelve-year-old daughter.

"They become your slaves for life," Poontang said. "Girls that age haven't been corrupted yet. You can teach them everything; how to suck cock properly, how to clean up the dishes, go out and get jobs, everything. And they'll do it." But he went on and on so much about it that Plover finally calmed himself down and asked, rather sarcastically, "Listen, how old was the youngest girl you ever balled?"

Poontang looked at him with feigned surprise. "Twelve."

"Yeah? And how old were you at the time?"

"Nine."

"You mean to tell me you got your first piece of ass when you were *nine years old?*"

"No. You asked me about the youngest girl I ever balled. That was when I was nine. Before that I had to do with some slightly older broads."

Plover did not know what to believe.

33

Captain Poontang did not have a job. He owned the houseboat on which he lived, and moorage was a few dollars a month including electricity, gas, and water. If Plover wanted to be harsh about it, Captain Poontang was a thief, a beggar, and a chronic borrower.

Inside the abandoned ferryboat to which Poontang's boat was moored were two cavernous empty areas, which had been used to store automobiles when the ferry had crossed the bay from San Francisco to Oakland. Now, in between these tunnels, was a big box full of old clothes and shoes. People around Gate Five who were abandoning something would dump it in the box. People who wanted clothes would rummage through it until they found something attractive or their size. Most nights one or more homeless young people would sleep in among the clothing. This is where Poontang got most of the clothes he owned. The rest were either left over from his New York days or given to him by women.

Women also gave him most of his food and money. Plover could not understand why women seemed to find Poontang attractive enough to give him anything, much less sleep with him. But they did. And not just the girls around Gate Five, either. More than once Plover had been sitting with friends in the Old Town Saloon and seen Poontang enter the bar on the arm of an attractive, well-dressed woman. Poon would always have a smile and a wink for Plover, but he would take his lady to another table. "Women like to be concentrated on before they fuck," he told Plover one day. But they did more than fuck. They would come down to the houseboat with sacks of groceries or their husband's cast-off clothes (most of which would end up in the Free Box), bottles of wine, and sometimes even cash. "I don't care what you bring, as long as you bring your bird," Poon said to a woman in front of Plover one afternoon. Plover started to be embarrassed, but the woman was not and Plover realized that as vulgar and crude as Poon was nobody seemed to mind much. Maybe it was because he was so easy about it.

Poontang was also on welfare part of the time and received food stamps. He could not buy cat food on the food stamps, so Thomas P. Wetherby had to eat stew beef. "Government regulations are turning my cat into a gourmet," Poon said. "Hah hah."

And sometimes there were no more food stamps, and no women showed up, and everybody else seemed broke at the same time. Then, for food, Captain Poontang would have to cruise the supermarkets. Since he was ragged, long-haired, and bearded, he could not get away with the middle-class shopper's methods of loading up a cart and eating a lot of food before getting to the check stand. He had to actually sneak the food out of the market. Always he stole dry cat food first and then he tried the meat counters. If he could get away with much meat, he would put the dry cat food back, not out of any sense of honor, but because the dry cat food was bulky. "You would be surprised at how much meat you can stuff down your pants," he told Plover.

If they had food and shelter, Poontang didn't much care about anything else. He was never short of marijuana or pills because people gave them to him. He did not drink much (only, in fact, when someone would buy him a drink) and poverty had helped him to quit smoking tobacco.

Plover tried to explain to Captain Poontang that he was something of a parasite. "Don't talk to me," Poon said. "Talk to the people living on inheritances." Another time he said, "I figure the world owes me a living."

"Why?" Plover asked, because he knew he was expected to.

"Figure it this way. I feel I got a natural talent as a leader of men, you know what I mean? Now, if I developed that talent, worked at it, polished myself up and all that shit, then I'd become a great leader or general or something like that. In my capacity as a leader, I would lay waste to thousands of miles of land, kill thousands of people, torture guys, shoot babies, all that crap. As it is, I don't do any of these things. The world is a better place, thanks to me, hah hah."

It was twilight, and Gate Five was calm and beautiful. Patches of yellow and amber light came from the quiet houseboats, where people made their dinners or sat at tables eating them. The bay glistened around the boats, and Plover could hear distant laughter coming from one of the boats tethered out in the bay. He did not want to go back to his motel room or down to Sausalito. He did not want to sit in a restaurant alone eating dinner, and he did not want to go to the Old Town Saloon and pick up a dinner companion. He knew they would all be there. It was practically a club. The people who had no one to go home to or no one to stay home for. Plover was one of them, and he ate with them more than he ate alone. The women of the group were all in their thirties or forties, most of them divorced, and for some reason without their children; the men were bachelors or divorced, between girlfriends or wives, and all of them were bored with their own company. Plover knew he had to eat, and he knew that eating was a social ritual, but he wished there was some way it could be avoided for a day or two. He wished he had his own apartment. Then he could go home and cook his own supper and either read or watch television. He did not want to take a sandwich to the motel and watch television. It seemed sort of dirty.

On the other hand, Plover did not want to stay with Captain Poontang or offer to buy his dinner. It would seem too much like paying for his company. Plover knew how valuable Poon had been to him for the past couple of weeks, as a companion and conversationalist. He had helped Plover to stop thinking about himself, and to look into another way of living, a way totally foreign to Plover. But not tonight.

He said good-bye to Poon and petted the cat and went aboard the ferry. It was dark inside the tunnel, and Plover walked gingerly, trying to avoid stepping in dog shit. As he passed the Free Box he saw a tall shadowy figure rising up out of the heaps of clothing. The figure seemed to be a wild-haired man wearing a blanket. Plover walked a little faster, opened the gate, and walked down the catwalk to land. His Volkswagen was parked in the rutty dirt not far from the ferryboat, among the other cars. When Plover got to it he saw a young man shutting the door of his, Plover's, car.

"Looking for something?" Plover said. He was frightened. The young man was thin and mean-looking in the darkness.

"Fuck you," the young man said. He started backing away. Plover tried to think if there was anything in his car worth stealing. No. He could not think of a thing.

"Have a good day," he said ironically to the young man. That was what hitchhikers said when they got out of your car. The young man muttered something that sounded nasty and moved off among the cars. Plover got inside his car and started the engine and got out of there. Once on the Sausalito road he relaxed. The kid was probably a speed freak. They get pretty mean. Plover found out when he parked the car in Sausalito and looked in the glove compartment that the kid had taken all the Blue Chip Stamps. That was all right. Plover never used them anyway.

34

He was still thinking of the irony of a speed freak with Blue Chip Stamps when he entered the Old Town Saloon. Another Sunday night in the Old Town Saloon. There they all were. Plover edged his way through the noisy crowd. There was no place for him to sit or stand at the bar. He looked around the room. He did not see anybody he wanted to sit with. His skin began to warm as he saw himself going home to the motel this early. No place for Plover. He turned and faced the bar again and saw Tony waving at him. He waved back stoically, but Tony persisted. Plover edged his way in to the bar. Tony said, "Thalia called here for you. She has some message."

Plover went to the front of the bar and waited outside the telephone alcove while a young girl pleaded with

somebody. "Please," she said. "Oh, please . . . please."
Plover tried not to listen. He was glad the girl was in
there, because it gave him time to straighten out his
thoughts. Thalia was not calling him because she wanted
to talk to him. She had a message, and she felt it was important enough to get in touch with him this way. His
best act would be to calmly accept the idea of talking to
her as a friend who has a message, not as a husband or
lover. That was the way to play it. Good old Plover, calling for his message. He even toyed with the idea of saying
he had called to say hello to the children. But that would
be fake. He *would* ask to speak to them, though.

The girl was still urgently moaning "Please," into the
telephone. With some irritation Plover ordered a beer
from the waitress and stood against the wall sipping it,
waiting. At last the girl came out of the alcove. Plover
looked to see if she had tears in her eyes, but could see
none.

The message was nothing urgent. Thalia had meant to
tell him before. He had been invited to a cocktail party
at the Fairmont Hotel that night, in honor of Manny Delasko. She thought he would want to go, but it seemed too
late now.

"No," Plover said. "These things go on half the night.
I'd kind of like to go. When did the invitation come?"

"Oh, a couple of weeks ago. Right after you got back
from New York."

"I think I'll go," Plover said. He paused, and the telephone made distant buzzing and popping noises. "Listen," he said, "would you like to go with me? I mean, I'd
be your escort, nothing else." He was thinking that
Thalia might want to go to this thing. A lot of important

people would be there, and she could wear one of her expensive dresses.

"I don't think it would be right," she said. "Thank you anyway."

"Okay," he said, and paused again. "Oh, Christ, my suit. Hey. Ha ha, listen, could you press my suit? It's still in my suitcase at the motel."

Plover arrived at the Fairmont Hotel dressed in his dark brown suit, vest, bright yellow shirt and gold accessories. He had drunk two bottles of Dos Equis while he waited for Thalia to press both the suit and the shirt, and then in a warm glow of companionship kissed her on the cheek and squeezed her as he left. Now he felt just fine. The party was going to be full blast (it was after ten o'clock) with lots of pretty women. He walked through the lobby and down the carpeted corridor to the room where the party was being held. There was a crowd at the door, around the little card table where a woman was checking invitations. Plover spotted Herb Caen the columnist in the group, and he ducked around them. He did not want to talk to Caen, because he did not want news of his separation to hit the paper. He knew it was quite possible that Caen and the public would not be interested, but he didn't want to take the chance. By avoiding Caen, he avoided the woman checking invitations, although he had his own in his pocket, and so felt as if he had crashed. It was a good feeling. The room was full of noise and people; just the way he liked it. On the left side of the room was a long white-clothed table loaded down with food. At one end three liveried bartenders passed out drinks. Plover made directly for the bartenders.

When his turn came he winked at the bartender before him and said, "Straight out of the bottle bourbon."

The bartender grinned and poured a triple shot in a wide glass. "Don't get many calls for *that*, sir," he said. Happily certain he had impressed the bartender, Plover moved off through the crowd. All the big shots were there, especially the radio and television people. Manny Delasko had been one of them, a bright young radio and then television personality on the local scene who had luckily volunteered to m.c. the pilot of a half-hour game show which had luckily clicked, and now Manny was off to film twenty-six segments in Hollywood. The cocktail party was not so much a farewell as an acknowledgment of status, and it was being paid for by the game-show producers. Plover had to ask several people the name of the show before he found out. "Bet Your Bundles." Plover winced. Aimed at housewives, he supposed. Bundles, snicker snicker.

He saw Manny across the room by the windows overlooking the city, talking to Don Sherwood and Ronnie Schell. Plover decided to avoid them for the present and went back to the bar for another drink. A girl he knew slightly, who worked at the San Francisco Museum, caught hold of him, and he joined her little group for a few minutes, bolting his drink, laughing at her jokes, putting his arm around her waist and hugging her, and finally going back to the bar for another one when the girl's boyfriend showed up. To the bartender Plover said, "Gotta drink up this free hooch fast as I can!" The bartender agreed.

"Franklin Plover, you darling man!" he heard a low

female voice say with obvious delight. He turned around and found himself looking down into a pair of large brown eyes. He did not know the girl. She was wearing a dress cut to show most of her snowy white breasts. She reached out a hand for one of Plover's and he squeezed back, but she still did not let go. "I bet you don't remember me," she said.

"I can't recall your face, but those tits are unmistakable, hee hee," he said. She looked shocked at first, and when he kept giggling and squeezing her hand, she made a pretty little face and said, "You naughty man! How dare you talk to me like that!"

"You're the one with the sexy dress," he said. "Not me."

"But I bet you can't remember where we met, can you?"

"As a matter of fact, no. Did we meet someplace?"

A man with an old face and an obvious hairpiece, wearing a plaid dinner jacket, came up to them and put his hand on the girl's elbow. "Oh, Timmy, I want you to meet Franklin Plover, you know, the man on the radio in the morning."

The man held out a weary hand and said, "Roxbury."

Plover said, giggling, "Is that your name, or what's making you so sick?" Roxbury laughed, looking elsewhere, murmured something to the girl, and moved off through the crowd. Plover said, "Is that your escort?"

"Not really. He's just money."

"What do you mean, Just money?"

"You know, no talent or anything."

"What's your name?"

They made their way back to the bar and she told

Plover her name was Jennie Starkweather and she was a photographer's representative. She drank Scotch with a little water. She and Plover had met a couple of years before at a similar cocktail party for Lena Horne when her autobiography came out. Plover remembered the party very well. He and Thalia had gotten super-smashed and later had been thrown out of the Trident for shushing the musicians. To blur this memory he said to Jennie, "I bet I can eat fifty stuffed eggs."

"Oh, I saw that movie," she said, but he took her arm and moved her down to a tray of stuffed eggs. He picked one up, glared at it, and popped it into his mouth. "One," he said, after swallowing it. That, as it turned out, was his entire dinner.

The party was a great success for Plover. He met and talked with a lot of San Francisco people he hadn't seen in a long time, many of them professional acquaintances from before his success with the talk show. It amused him to be fawned over by people who once had little or no time for him, and everywhere he went at the party there was laughter, much of it his. He kept one eye out for Jennie Starkweather, as she, too, moved from group to group. When they were both in the same group he would reach out and hold her hand, squeezing it and smiling fondly at her. She seemed to like it. She never took her hand away. Plover began to believe that he would spend the night with her. He did not even bother to ask. He knew. That was all there was to that. Meanwhile there was plenty of free liquor and plenty of nice people to talk to. He began to wish he had brought Captain Poontang along. Poon would have loved the party, and the party would have loved him.

Eventually, Jennie Starkweather came up to him and pulled him gently aside. "We have to go to a supper," she said. "I've been asked to invite you to come with us. Will you?"

"To be with you, I'd go to a *dozen* supper parties," he said.

"Oh, you're so funny." She wrote the address down for him on the inside of a matchbook and tucked it into one of his vest pockets. "I have my own car, so I'll see you over there. In about half an hour?"

"Sure. Then you and me can go to your place, right?"

He knew he was leering at her, but everything was in a rosy glow of happiness and erotic anticipation, and he did not care. She leered back at him, anyway. "Of course, sweety," she said.

Plover's car was in the garage across California Street from the Fairmont. It was cold out, the wind blowing from the west, fog clinging to the lights and glowing from the cablecar tracks. Plover hurried across the street, sobering just slightly. He drove carefully down the hill and across town to Telegraph Hill. Every street in North Beach was congested with cars. Plover drove carefully up the streets and down the streets, but he could not find a parking place. It was one of those nights. Finally, he crossed Columbus Avenue and went up Union Street to the top of Russian Hill and parked in the residential section. It was a long walk back down to North Beach and up Telegraph, but Plover enjoyed it, once the exercise made him warm enough.

The apartment was on Montgomery Street, on the fashionable side of the hill, with a fantastic view of the bay and the east bay hills and cities. Plover stood out on the front steps enjoying the view and catching his breath for a few minutes, vaguely hearing the babble of voices from within. At last he pressed the doorbell and was admitted by a man who called him "Plov," and patted him on the back.

This second party was not as much fun as the first. Everyone was overdressed and stood or sat around with paper plates of food. The liquor was served in thin plastic glasses, and Plover suspected that their host had collected the glasses from airplane flights. The apartment was expensively furnished, but a cheap streak dominated everything; there were first editions on the shelves, but they were cheap first editions, obviously (to Plover anyway) collected by a man who wanted first editions rather than books. One of the papyrus plumes in the urn beside the fireplace was broken. The tabletops and other wooden surfaces had been sprayed with plastic, so that glasses could not make rings. To Plover this was the cheapest yet. Their host was the man who had called him "Plov," and so he was not feeling charitable toward him anyway.

Plover did not feel like eating. He drank rapidly from his plastic glass, noting that the bourbon was cheap enough to burn his throat. He did not participate much in the conversation. All he wanted to do was get hold of Jennie Starkweather and get her to her softly lit apartment and climb in bed with her. She, on the other hand, seemed to be enjoying herself. She was sitting on the floor surrounded by men, talking and laughing, while Plover was across the room on his feet. He kept trying to catch her eye, but she would not look toward him. She had hardly spoken to him since he had come in. Maybe she was changing her mind. Maybe one of these yahoos had a claim on her. He did not like any of the people here. They all seemed to be stockbrokers or advertising people. They were talking righteously about marijuana, which they felt should be legalized.

"I guess you could say you represented the *long-hairs* around here, Plov," the host said. "What's your opinion on legalizing pot?"

Plover did not think his hair was all that long, but only just long enough for these cruds to think he was a long-hair. Fortunately, he had some opinions on the subject. He grinned crookedly, like Errol Flynn, and said, "I think it ought to be legal to possess and use, but there ought to be a mandatory death sentence for selling it. Is what I think."

White faces looked at him blankly. Not a black man in the room. *Where is your token spook?* Plover wanted to ask the faces.

One of the women, wearing a long red dress, said to him, "But, aren't you against capital punishment?"

Plover grinned crookedly again. "Not for dope dealers."

A heavy man who must have been hell on the football fields of yesteryear stood up and said, "You don't really classify marijuana, or pot, among the dangerous drugs, do you?"

Several murmurs of agreement came from the others. Jennie, however, was just smiling. She listened to him on the air. She knew pretty much where he stood. Although, come to think of it, he had tried to conceal his feelings on the air; he could not imagine why. "Look," he said. "Marijuana, or shit, as we used to call it when I was a boy, is easy to grow. There's no reason anybody should have to buy or sell it. All the trouble comes when you start selling the stuff. It's up to twelve dollars a lid, right now. With that money drug dealers are getting fat and rich. They don't give credit. They take cash. All the cash is going to the dope freaks. But that's beside the point. If shit were free, those motherfuckers on Madison Avenue wouldn't ever be able to get their hands on it. Can't you see what would happen if dope was legalized without protecting us from Madison Avenue? We'd be paying fifty cents a pack for marijuana adulterated with tobacco. Our children would see it on television, 'Ahh, take a puff and disappear!' Another bullshit product for the bullshit machine. Better we should execute a few dealers."

"I must say, that's a unique position," the football player said. He turned away from Plover and started a conversation with somebody Plover could not see. Laying on the old trip to Coventry, he thought.

"Hey, let's stop talking about it and smoke some!" the woman in red said. But nobody seemed to have any marijuana to smoke. "Oh, what a shame," somebody said. "No hope without dope!" That got a big laugh. Plover was disgusted. Next they'd start talking about group sex or wife-swapping, and then they'd start talking about their ministers. He had been to these parties before.

"Hey," he said, not very loudly. "I go get us some fucking dope. Stay where you are." He left the party, feeling the cold delightful shock of the fog against his face. His vest felt tight across his stomach, and although the wind made his jacket flap, he did not try to button it. He was still too fat. As he glided flapping down the hill into North Beach he thought about losing some weight, jogging, perhaps, or dynamic tension in the bathroom. The idea was to get into some kind of physical shape. He would soon be forty, and it would be too late. Too late, old man. Life passing you by. Grant Street. Crowded with tourists and mean rotten hippies and street people. Plover walked down Grant toward the apex of Broadway and Columbus, being jostled by funseekers. He thought he would go down to Vesuvio's and get a couple of beers. There ought to be some friendly faces at Vesuvio's, even though the owner sold the place a couple of years before. He used to hang out there in the old days. Surely some of the old crowd would still be around. Suddenly he did not want to see them. Fuck the old crowd, and fuck himself for sentimentally wanting to see them. Whoever they were, a bunch of drunken blurry faces from the sixties. Even the fifties. He abruptly turned right and walked down the hill, past a screaming faggot bar. He paused in front of the lights from a pool hall. He could hear the friendly click of the billiard balls inside. He was fond of that sound and he smiled. That sound had pleasant memories. He had been a hell of a player back in college, and before that he had hung around pool halls enough to know the ropes. He was an old pool hall boy. He stepped inside.

It was not an old-fashioned pool hall. It was one of those places that opened after *The Hustler* made pool popular again, with peach-colored felt on the rickety tables, and a soda bar, and plenty of fancy decorations to attract the ladies. This one, though, in the heart of North Beach, was shabby and rundown, the peach-colored felt faded and stained, the balls dirty, the carpeting torn and badly stained by vomit, liquor, soft drinks, ice cream, and probably blood. Plover did not see any white people in the room; only some Chinese in the back, and at the tables in front of him, black young men and women. The boys seemed to be about eighteen or nineteen, and terribly black. The girls appeared to be younger, and Plover guessed that they might be prostitutes. One of them, dressed in a black leather jacket and lavender mini, with black boots, said, "Get your white ass out of here, motherfucker." The other girls and boys laughed at him.

"That's easy to say," Plover said. "You're probably a tough revolutionary with a knife. I just came in here to prove something."

"What you want to prove?" the same girl said. She tilted her head to one side caustically.

"I have a fifty dollar bill in my pocket," Plover said. He leaned easily against one of the tables and took one of the balls out of the rack and rolled it down into a pocket. "I just wanted to find out if anybody in here could beat me at pool. For fifty."

The girl said, "Shiiit!" but one of the boys moved forward and said, "What you play best?" Then he added, "Whitey."

"Don't give me any of that Whitey crap," Plover said. "There isn't any of that shit in the game of pool. In pool only two things count—how much money you have and how well you play. No race war, no prejudice, no bullshit."

The black young man seemed to get very tense. He said, "What's your best game?"

"I play all games equally well," Plover said. "But I don't play you."

"You chickenshit!" one of the girls said. The boy who wanted to play pool looked around grinning.

Plover said, "Because you don't have the fifty bucks. Do you?"

"Listen, you son of a bitch," the kid started, but Plover interrupted.

"I said, don't give me that shit. I don't have to listen to it. You know why I don't have to listen to it? Because I can play better pool than you, and I have the money to back up the play."

"I'll play you for two dollars on the nine," the kid said.

"Fuck that shit," Plover said. "We could die of old age before somebody made any money. One game of one-pocket for fifty dollars. *Now.*"

The kid looked frustrated and angry, but he also looked disappointed, and so Plover decided to leave him alone. To the first girl who had spoken to him he said, "You see? You see *where it's at?*" He hoped he got enough irony into the phrase. He didn't want her to misunderstand him. The five or six black kids were silent. Plover smiled his Errol Flynn smile and walked out of the place.

Outside he snickered. He did not have fifty dollars or anything like it. They seemed like nice kids, the same kind of kids he had known when he was a kid. Really interested in pool. Otherwise they could have ganged up on him and taken his nonexistent fifty dollars. He walked back up past the fag joint, thinking, I must not think of that place as a fag joint. *Gay Bar,* that's the phrase. He thought about going in, but decided against it. You never know who you're going to run into in one of those places. Hee hee. Better to go back to Sausalito, where he had plenty of friends. He would get to the Old Town Saloon in time for last call, if he hurried.

He turned around and headed for Russian Hill, passing the pool hall once again. He waved at the shadows in the windows, hoping they could see it was him, and then hurried on. After all, when you stop and think about it, those kids had every right to come out and righteously kill him.

Plover was on the Golden Gate Bridge, making pretty good time but staying within the speed limits, when he realized that Thalia would probably be in the saloon. He did not know why he knew, he just knew. She came in there once in a while. And tonight she had refused to go out with him. So she would be there, thinking he was somewhere else. Well, he would show her that he was not somewhere else, and that the Old Town Saloon was his property, not hers. She had her goddamned nerve, skulking in and out of that place when she thought he wouldn't be around. God damn her fucking ass. He would show her.

Plover parked in the lot on the bay side of Bridgeway and hurried across the damp foggy street to the Old Town Saloon. He knew how drunk he was, but he did not care. He had worked up a rage against Thalia, an almost joyful feeling of release. He did not understand it and he did not want to. He only wanted to vindicate himself.

Inside the bar only two or three customers remained at the tables in the front. Ted the bartender looked up and saw Plover and grinned in such a way that Plover knew he was right. In the back of the bar he saw Thalia sitting beside a man. There was no one else in that section of the bar, so they were together. Plover stood in front of them, looking only at Thalia. Her eyes were large and startled.

"I'm sick of this civilized shit," Plover said loudly. "Get outside!"

"All right, all right," Thalia said. She started to get up, and the man next to her stood also. Plover looked at him. He had a gentle face and mild eyes.

"You get the fuck out of here," Plover said to him.

"Okay," the man said, and vanished from Plover's sight. Plover took hold of Thalia's arm and pushed her into the aisle. "Move it," he said roughly. "Civilized crap! It just means I stand around and let everybody, including you, *shit* on me! *Fuck* it! Fuck *you!* You're my *wife* and that's *that!*"

"Don't push me," she said. They were at the door. He pushed her through the door and she said "Ouch! You're hurting me!" By now they were on the sidewalk. He took her by the arm and pushed her out into the street.

"Hurt you," he said. "Don't you know how you've hurt *me?*" Suddenly it was more than he could stand. He pulled her around to face him, and with a burst of joy he swung on her. *"You bitch!"* He hit her on the mouth. She yelled and went down.

"Oh my God," Plover said.

"Don't you touch me, goddamn you!" Thalia yelled. She got up. "POLICE!!"

"Aw," Plover said. "You don't have to do that. Don't you know I didn't mean it?"

"You're crazy drunk! You keep away from me! PO-LICE!!"

"Aw." Plover started feeling sad. He walked over to his car and leaned against it, waiting for the police. He heard Thalia say, "It's all right. Here come the police."

He could hear the police radio, and then the murmuring of a conversation between Thalia and a policeman. Soon the policeman walked over toward him, and Plover lifted his head. He was crying.

"The little lady's going home," the policeman said. "Why don't we get in my car and talk about it?"

"Okay," Plover said. "But I'm sure goddamn sorry you got involved."

The officer sighed. "That's all right. I'm used to it."

"I'm not," Plover said. They got into the police car, and Plover started crying again. "Oh, God damn," he sobbed. "I just hate like hell to cry in front of somebody."

"It's all right," the policeman said. "She your wife?"

"Yes." Plover blew his nose into a Kleenex the officer gave him.

"I know what it's like for you," the officer said. He seemed to be a man of about fifty. "But you have to stay away from her. You can't go hitting her on the street. No matter how you feel."

"I know. You know, I never ever hit her before. In all the years we were married. Never once."

"That's how it goes," the officer said.

"I thought maybe if I hit her everything would be okay. Isn't that insane?"

"Thoughts like that do occur to people," the officer said. "You've been drinking quite a bit lately. Screws up the mind."

"I guess it does."

The officer looked at his watch. "Well, I guess the little lady's well on her way home by now. Will you give me your word you won't follow her?"

"Yes, officer," Plover said. "Listen, you've been pretty damned nice to me."

"Well, I know how you feel," the officer said. "You can go now."

Plover got out of the police car and very carefully walked in a sober manner to his car, got in, and soberly drove away. To the motel. He called his house. After four rings, Thalia answered.

"Honey," he said. "Are you all right?" Her voice sounded muffled.

"You split my lip," she said. "You stay away from me. You're crazy."

"I can't stay away. I have to come over. I can't let it end like this. I have to come over."

"Don't you dare come over here."

"Can I come over in the morning?"

"You can call me in the morning. We'll see. Right now you better get to sleep. You should see a doctor. You're crazy."

"I'm so *sorry*," he said miserably, but she hung up. He went out and got into his car and drove to Mill Valley.

He parked down on the street and walked quietly up the driveway to the front door. With his key he unlocked the door. The lights were on in the living room. Thalia stood there, wearing her bathrobe. Her mouth was swollen and split, bloody and terrible-looking. Plover wanted to laugh hysterically. Instead he said very quietly, "I'm sober now. I had to come over. We have to make some kind of peace."

Weary and sad, Thalia sat down. "All right," she said. "I suppose we do."

35

Plover went into the kitchen and got himself a glass of water. The kitchen was a mess. Back in the living room he sat down and sipped at his water, watching Thalia as she dabbed tenderly at her lip with a pink-stained Kleenex.

"Who was that guy you were sitting with?" he asked.

"Is that how we're going to make peace?"

"No, I just wondered how it was you were there with him and I seemed to know about it. I was wondering if he was a friend of yours, or maybe he was trying to pick you up or something."

"He's a friend."

"Have you known him long?"

"I'm not going to answer your questions. I don't have to."

"But I think I have a right to know if you were going out with him before we split up."

"Not him, no."

"But somebody else."

"No. I'm not going to answer your questions. You might as well leave. I know how sorry you are that you hit me. But I'm afraid of you. I think I've been afraid of you for years. You have to see a doctor. There might be something *organic* wrong with you."

"I don't know what you're talking about. What have I done that's so crazy?"

Thalia glared at him over her split lip.

"Oh, listen," he said. "I only hit you once, one time. Lots of guys hit their wives all the time. That's not crazy."

"I never saw you like that before."

"How come we're talking about me? You're the one who wants to end the marriage. All I want is for us to get back together."

"You certainly don't act like it."

"How do you want me to act? For Christ's sake! I have feelings! I can't just sit around waiting for you to make up your mind! I'm going out of my mind! I want to come home!"

"Is that why you're living in a motel?"

"What?"

"Are you living in a motel because you expect me to call up on the telephone some night and ask you to come home?"

He looked at her. She was starting to cry. She angrily

pulled another Kleenex from the box on her lap and held it to her nose.

"Of course not," Plover said weakly. "We were going to wait six months, weren't we, before we made any decision? I don't want to move back in here now."

"I don't want to wait six months," Thalia said. Her voice and her eyes were full of emotion. *"I want out!"*

Plover sat watching her cry while the words reached in and made themselves part of him. At last he believed her. He could not understand how he had managed to fool himself all these months. It did not make any difference if Thalia had or did not have a boyfriend, or whether Plover stayed away and let her think things out, or if he forcefully took control and moved back in, daring her to move out. It would not matter if they saw doctors, lawyers, or counselors. It was over.

He wanted to touch her or kiss her before he left, but he knew that this was not the time. There would be time later, after they could become friends again. He had missed her friendship, he now realized, and he wanted it back.

"I'll leave now," he said softly, and stood up. She watched him, still crying and still wary. He waved his hand stupidly from the door, opened it and went out and down the driveway to his car. He looked at his watch. It was three-thirty. He had to be at work in three hours, and there would be no sleep for him. He got into the car, started the engine, and drove to the station parking lot in Sausalito. He sat in the car thinking until the engineer arrived, and then they both went inside and had coffee.

36

"Good morning, this is Plover."

"Uh, hello?"

"Yes, go ahead. This is Plover."

"Is this Plover? Am I on the air?"

"That's right. This is Plover and we are both on the air. What would you like to talk about?"

"Are you sure?"

"Am I sure what?"

"Are you sure this is Plover? You don't sound the same."

"But I feel the same, Caller. Now what's your question?"

"Did you see this morning's *Chronicle?*"

"No. Good morning, this is Plover."

"Huh? Is this Plover?"

"That's right, Ma'am."

"What happened to the man you were just talking to?"

"Turn your radio down, Ma'am. We're on six-second delay. You know that. You've called before."

"Well you still didn't answer that man's question."

"He didn't ask one. Good morning. This is Plover."

"Boy, Plover, you have no idea how long I been trying to reach you. Weeks!"

"Well, you finally made it. What's your question?"

"Hey, you sound different. Anything the matter?"

"Nope. Good morning, this is Plover."

"My, we're being blunt this morning. Now, don't interrupt! I want to see what your other callers think about these Weathermen. I mean, it's one thing to protest against the establishment. And quite another thing to go around planting bombs where they might injure innocent people. What do you think?"

"Don't ask me, lady. I haven't got the guts to crucify a frog, much less bomb a police station."

"Well, I mean, can't you see a difference between open warfare and sneaking around planting bombs?"

"Which side are you on, Lady?"

"Now you can't tell me those maniacs shouldn't be locked up and throw away the key! They've—"

"I wouldn't even try, Lady. You go on back to your tranquilizers. Good morning, this is Plover."

"I would like. Hello? I would like to respond to the lady's question concerning the Weathermen faction of the Students for a Democratic Society, if I might."

"Nobody's stopping you."

"Well, it's pretty clear to me that these revolutionary

fellows haven't taken history into consideration. You know, those who fail to study history are doomed to repeat it. But these young people mistake Kropotkin's actions even after fifty or sixty years! Can't they see that bombings function purely to awaken the masses to their state? That death of humans is never the actual goal, merely a symbolic reference—"

"Good morning, this is Plover."

"What'd you eat, nails for breakfast? Whew! Are you tough this morning!"

"Oh, hi. Wee bit of a hangover, old pal. Wee bit of a hangover."

"Gee, Plover, I didn't know you drank. Anyhow, let me respond, too. I think it's okay for the Weathermen to blow up police stations, just so long as all they kill are policemen. You get my meaning?"

"I think so. No innocent civilians, hey?"

"That's it. We all know the police are the enemy. Hey, I got a sure-fire cure for a hangover."

"What is it?"

"Get drunk! Haw haw!"

"My pal. Hello, this is Plover."

"What on earth was the matter with that man? Killing policemen isn't going to solve anything!"

"Except maybe for policemen's wives. Good morning, this is Plover, and don't let's talk about bombs or Weathermen, okay?"

"Hello? Am I on?"

"You're on, darling. Speak."

"I've been sitting here for twenty minutes. My arm is killing me."

"Everybody in Northern California sympathizes with you. What's your question?"

"Well, I wanted to talk about those Weathermen, but you said no, so I guess I'll use my time to talk about Ronnie Reagan. I think he's the worst governor the state of California has ever had. He must hate people."

"He's also the most popular governor California's ever had. Does this mean anything to you?"

"What's the matter with you this morning? You're not your usual cheerful self. Oh, hangover, but I don't believe that."

"You'd better, Sweets. Good morning, this is Plover."

"I'm going to kill you."

"Cut him off the tape. Good morning, this is Plover."

"Oh, Mister Plover, I've been a fan of yours for ever so long. And now at last I get to speak to you. I must tell you, I have a little trouble with my sleep, these last few years, and so I've come to rely on my radio quite a bit. I don't see well enough for the television, oh, I listen sometimes, but mostly the radio. I'm the only one up at this hour of the morning, and so I can listen to you with the telephone here on my lap in the living room, oh, I must be just talking on and on. I really did have a question for you. Now, what was it? I didn't realize you could get stage fright talking on the telephone. Oh, I just can *not* remember that question!"

"Are you really an old woman, or is this a put-on?"

"A put-on? I don't quite understand what you mean."

"Whatever you are, you almost had me crying there. I cry like a bandit when I've got a hangover. Hear that, folks? Your old dad has a hangover. It's so bad I'm talking like a disk jockey, fans. Just to keep from throwing up. It hardly seems worth it. Good morning, this is Plover."

"Ronald Reagan is *not* the most popular governor California ever had. I'm ashamed of you, Plover. The most popular Governor was Earl Warren, who served for eight years—"

"Don't tell me about Earl Warren, mister. I lived in California then, as a child, and people on the streets were whispering about Earl Warren. Sure, they voted for him, but they didn't like him. He dressed corny. Good morning, this is Plover."

"Boy, you're really *something* this morning!

"And you're nothing any morning. Good morning, this is Plover."

"Hey, man, you're blowing your cool. You're talking down to your friends, man. You got to get your head in a better place—"

"Don't talk to me in that hip oatmeal jargon, buster. If you have something to say, say it in English, if you can remember any English."

"Man, you sure get uptight about language. I bet you don't like long hair, either."

"It makes me sick, except on women. Then I can dig it. Good morning, this is Plover."

"Aha, my little shore bird, and how are we this fine and happy morning? Did we take a little spin on the golden wheel of dame alcohol? Are we suffering just a teeny bit from the remorse that attacks gods and men alike? Hmmm?"

"Thanks for the sympathy. Do you have a question, or did you call up merely to jostle me?"

"A question for the younger generation: Young ladies and gentlemen, kindly remember that myself and an entire generation of sots and ne'er-do-wells were sniffing cocaine before your mothers met your fathers. It is only because of ruinous reverses on the stock market that I do not continue my nose-candy habit. Finances aren't what they used to be."

"What do you drink these days, Pop?"

"Sweet wine, my lad."

"Well, don't hock your radio. Good morning, this is Plover."

"What I can't understand is why you allow so much air time to old fools like that, and when people call up with serious questions you cut them off."

"Good morning, this is Plover."

"Did you cut that person off?"

"Good morning, this is Plover."

"Am I on the air?"

"You are indeed."

"I have a question for your listeners."

"We wait with bated breath."

"Assuming that there was a revolution between blacks and whites. Which side would you be on?"

"Say, that's a tricky question, Caller. You mean to trap people, don't you? By reducing the issue to black and white, you're saying that all the black people will have to be on one side, and all the white people on the other. Isn't that right, Caller?"

"Well, doesn't that seem to you—"

"And of course we white people outnumber the hell out of the black people, right? And so the blacks had god-

219

damn better cool it, right? Or we whites will savage them, right? Good morning, this is Plover."

"I am a black man, and I wish to respond to that question."

"We are at your mercy."

"There is no war between blacks and whites in this country or anywhere else. There might be a war between *whites* and the other peoples of the world, but that is another matter. It is not as simple as black and white. There is an entire world out there composed of peoples who are neither black nor white, but brown, red, yellow, and many other colors. These peoples too have been exploited by the whites, and if a situation developed where open fighting had to break out, it would be the so-called Third World peoples against the whites. Then the whites would be outnumbered *fiercely*. That is what lies in the future, if present conditions are not remedied."

"I think I ought to tell you that while you were talking, I threw up into my waste basket. Good morning, this is Plover, bedraggled but ready to listen."

"Hello? Yes, I'm still waiting."

"You're on the air, mister. You can stop waiting. This is Plover."

"Oh, Frankie? How *are* you, my good friend!"

"Don't ask."

"Boy, you really told that guy. The one going on and on about them so-called third world people. Do you and him want to know why the so-called third world peoples haven't taken charge of things before now? It's because they don't have the initiative! It's as simple as that, isn't it?"

"Gosh, it sure sounds simple."

"Well, I mean, don't you agree? They'd be taking things easy and not making any trouble at all if it wasn't for certain outside agitators—"

"Outside? You mean they're not Americans?"

"Oh, come on, Plover, you know what I mean."

"I sincerely hope I don't. It begins to sound to me like the old party line, if you get my meaning."

"That's about the size of it."

"Not them, you. Good morning, this is Plover."

"Mmmmmmmmm!"

"Ah, it's you again. How are you this morning?"

"Mmmmmmmmmm!"

"You sound terrific. How about doing me a favor?"

"Mmmmmm?"

"You hum for a while, while I go get some more water. Okay?"

"Mmmmmmmmmmmmmmmmmmmmmmmmmmmmmmmmmmmmmmmmmmmm. Mmmmmmmmmmmmmmm."

"That's enough. Good morning, this is Plover."

"Hello, Plover?"

"That's right."

"Hey, you gone crazy or something? You're liable to lose your job. You've been talking nutty all morning."

"Let's just say I got tired of being the only sane person on the show, huh?"

"No, wait a minute. I think maybe you're drunk. That'd be a laugh, wouldn't it."

"I don't think it's funny. Good morning, this is Plover."

By now he felt so bad that it did not matter. Nothing mattered. Going on the air had been like coming out on stage; he had immediately forgotten the events of the past several hours under the pressure of being at work, and yet he could not bring himself up to his normal, careful stage presence. The engineer's booth was crowded with people. His engineer, his producer, Bob Hamilton, Peggy Lavan, looking concerned and sober, two hours early for work, and of course the boss, Fiedler, morose, a dead cigar jammed in the corner of his mouth. They looked like a jury behind glass. Plover was in too much pain to really care, but he wished they would go away. While an old tired-sounding woman complained about the street people in Berkeley (where she was raised), Plover drew in large black letters the words, "GO AWAY" on a napkin, and lifted it to the group in the booth. Only Peggy smiled, and nobody moved. Plover grinned at them and tore the napkin in half, punched out the old woman, and went on to the next caller.

He did not think he could last out the shift, but somehow he did. He leaned against the console while Peggy got her start, sipping a paper cup of coffee and wondering why he could not remember much about the night before. He had not been asleep. At least he thought he had not been asleep. When his mind was working better, he would have to think about it.

Peggy got to a record and turned to him. "Jesus, man. I turned you on this morning to listen while I got ready for work, and Jesus, you were really something. You sounded crazy. Are you all right?"

"Just a little tired, Plover said. "I stayed up all night."

"You really racked some ass," she said. "Are you quitting?"

"Quitting? Hell no. I can't afford to quit."

"Do you think he'll fire you?"

Plover grinned and leaned over the console, picking up Peggy's pack of Pall Malls. While Peggy watched him with raised eyebrows he shook out a cigarette and tucked it into the corner of his mouth.

"First one in six months," he said. He lit the cigarette. It tasted foul, but he inhaled deeply and felt the smoke hit. He was not worried about starting up again. He had quit once. It was easy. He blew the smoke out through his nose and said, "Well, wish me luck."

Fiedler and his producer Bob Hamilton were waiting for him in the hall. Plover stopped and said, "Listen, I don't want to hassle right now, okay?" He did not wait for an answer, but went on past. In the parking lot he looked down at himself in the sunlight, his suit frowsy and wrinkled, his vest unbuttoned, his yellow shirt flecked with tiny droplets of dried blood. He did not want to go to the motel, although he knew he should change clothes and take a shower. Oddly, he did not feel like sleeping at all now. He wondered if Captain Poontang was up yet. Maybe Poon would have some pills, or at least some marijuana. Anything to put off the hangover, which Plover knew from experience would be a humdinger.